Mistletowed

A HOLIDAY NOVELLA

Mistletowed

A HOLIDAY NOVELLA

ZARIAH L. BANKS

This is a work of fiction. Names, characters, organizations, places, events, and incidents are either products of the author's imagination or are used fictitiously. Any resemblance to actual persons, living or dead, or actual events is purely coincidental.

Published by eParke Press, Streetsboro, Ohio
Printed in the United States of America

ISBN 979-8-9869693-3-6 (ebook)
ISBN 979-8-9869693-4-3 (Print)
Library of Congress Control Number: 2024923407

Second Edition

Dedication

Dear reader, you're an important part of my journey.

Thanks for loving on my characters.

ZLB

Chapter One

"This cannot be my life right now," Mia groaned as she pulled her cowl neck scarf tighter around her neck, bracing against the crisp Brooklyn evening chill. She shivered so violently, her teeth chattered while panicked thoughts bounced in her head.

"Why didn't I just take the train tonight," she muttered as she paced back and forth in the small parking garage. She was so nervous that she could no longer sit inside her vehicle and wait. Leaning against her Honda, she checked her phone for what seemed like the fiftieth time. Roadside assistance had given her the tow truck's estimated arrival time, which was well over forty-five minutes ago. Her nerves were spent and couldn't spare much more time. An important meeting with a high-profile client was happening in less than—she checked her phone again—twenty-five minutes.

Just when she was contemplating calling an Uber, she noticed flashing orange and white lights dancing on the ceiling of the parking garage. She darted into the aisle and waved the tow truck driver over before he had time to call her. Although she wanted to cuss him out for leaving her waiting in the cold for so long, she knew his tardiness was likely out of his control. Besides, she was eager to get to the bottom of her car issue so she could get going. She was hanging onto hope that she could still make her nearby client appointment with a few minutes to spare.

The driver pulled up and stopped directly behind her sedan. After taking a few moments to gather his paperwork, he eased out of the truck's cab and strolled toward her, his casual pace making her bristle. He glanced at his clipboard, seemingly unbothered by her urgency. He was of average height with a stocky frame cloaked in a black down coat, dark jeans, and a crisp pair of Timbs.

Those kicks are too fresh for someone working in the snow and slush all day, she thought, rolling her eyes. She was so agitated that every little thing irked her.

Before looking away, she took in his strong cheekbones. The last thing she needed was to get distracted from her state of annoyance. Then his hazel eyes met hers and she took in the rest of his facial features. Her breath hitched with instant recognition. Is he Afro-Latino?

"Hello, Miss..." he glanced back down at his clipboard. "Reyes?"

She nodded. "That's me."

"Okay, good. I'm Preston with A. Gómez Towing. I apologize for the wait. There have been quite a few accidents this evening, with it being the first snowfall of the year."

"Hi, Preston. No problem and I'm so glad you're here. I was hoping you could give me a quick jump. I think my battery may have died while I was in my last meeting, and I have to get to my next one in a few minutes."

Preston gave a curt nod, then asked, "I see it's a 2008 Accord with nearly two hundred thousand miles on it." He whistled. "That's up there."

Mia sighed, nowhere near in the mood for a lecture about

the condition of her car. If she could have afforded a new one, she would have one. "Yes, it's an older car and often dies on me in extreme temperatures. And since it's only eighteen degrees this evening, here we are," she chuckled awkwardly. "But it should start right up with a quick jump, and I should be good to go in no time."

"A jump may last you for a little while, ma'am, but in this type of weather, the last thing you want is to be stuck with no transportation. Maybe you should look into other options if you get the opportunity down the road."

Now it was her time to give a curt nod. "Noted. Thanks."

She opened the back door, retrieved her purse, and handed over her license. Once he checked her ID and had her sign some paperwork, he began setting up the jumper cables. After a few unsuccessful attempts to jump her battery, Preston sighed. By then, Mia was shaking with nervous energy. A scream perched in her throat and she fought hard to choke it back.

She had recently returned to her hometown of Brooklyn after attending an interior design internship in Miami. Due to her recent relocation, she was rebuilding her client list. Just when her bank account was almost on fumes, a good friend of hers referred her to a small art gallery owner, Mr. Hardiman, who was interested in a redesign of his loft. He was he was on a tight deadline and was also considering another interior designer he'd interviewed the week before. Mia was counting on this opportunity to help her pay the rent for her apartment. But it looked like the meeting wouldn't be happening that evening.

"I'm sorry Miss Reyes, but you need your battery replaced." Preston glanced at her face, and his tone softened. "I can run you over to the auto parts store and install it for you. I'll have you on your way in under an hour."

She nodded numbly, holding back her tears. "Thank you, Preston. Just let me grab the rest of my things from the car."

On the way to the store, Mia called Mr. Hardiman and requested to reschedule their meeting.

"Mia, I'm sorry to hear about your current situation. But I don't think we'll need to reschedule. Johnathan, the other designer I met with, had a good understanding of the look I was going for. And I'm really in a rush to finish this project. So, for the sake of time, I think I'm going to move forward with him. I'll definitely keep you in mind should we ever need your services in the future."

"I see...well, thanks for the opportunity. And once again, I apologize for the inconvenience." She hung up the phone and stared out the window. She fought to breathe past the brick lying on her chest. Swiping at the fog-laden window, she bit her lip, refusing to cry in front of a perfect stranger.

Without this project, she didn't know how she would manage to keep her apartment. She could already hear her father asking her to move back in with him and her mother, wanting her to be his "precious niñita" forever.

Even though Brooklyn was her home, she'd left for an interior design internship, excited to find inspiration from a change of scenery and style. She was the baby of the family and her parents and siblings had all tried to talk her out of moving so far away. She'd just gotten settled down there when her sister, Emilia, found out she was pregnant with twins. While Mia was in Miami, she missed out on the first precious years of her twin niece and nephew's lives. To top it all off, her nephew, Harper, had been born with a congenital heart defect. She desperately wanted to be home to support her big sister during her difficult time. Instead, she'd made the tough decision to stay in the internship program, flew back home whenever she could, and video-chatted with her niece and nephew weekly once they were old enough to recognize her. Now that she was back in Brooklyn, she wanted nothing more than to splurge on expensive gifts for their first holiday season together. She felt like a total failure for not being able to support herself or give back to others during the most wonderful time of the year.

"Ms. Reyes?"

His velvety voice interrupted her thoughts. "Oh, I'm not used to responding to that. It's Mia."

"Mia," he said, pausing for a moment. "Sorry you had to cancel your meeting."

Yeah, me too. "Thanks, Preston, but you don't have to be. It wasn't your fault."

A few moments of silence passed between them before he asked, "So, you have that portfolio clutched to your chest like your life depends on it. What is it?"

Mia blinked, gazing down at her attaché case. She hadn't even realized she'd been doing that. "It's just my, um, designs."

His thick eyebrows raised. "You're an artist or something?"

She sniffed, then turned her attention back to the window, studying the passing city streets. "Or something."

"Makes sense. You look like the type."

She finally turned to look at him. "Oh, is that so? What type of artist do I look like?"

He seemed to think it over for a minute before responding. "Looks like you spent a lot of time on your makeup and your coat, boots, and hat are all completely different colors. But it all goes together nicely. So... I would guess something intricate like a fashion designer or a creator of mosaic art. Maybe using mixed media."

Mia studied his profile while he kept his eyes on the road, but she didn't respond.

When they made it to the auto parts store, Preston accompanied her inside and showed her which battery to select. At

5

the register, the cashier gave her the total and she reached into her purse for her wallet.

When she looked back up, the receipt was easing out of the printer and Preston was grabbing the bag.

"What are you doing?"

"Least I can do is buy this for you."

She started to protest, feeling a little awkward accepting it. She hated relying on someone, especially when she was already struggling to keep her life together. Accepting his help, especially with her finances so tight, made her feel vulnerable—but she couldn't afford to turn it down. "Thanks, I appreciate that."

On the ride back to her car, Preston asked, "Since you're not in a huge hurry anymore, can I suggest another detour to put a smile on your face?"

Chapter Two

Mia stared at Preston for a long moment before asking, "The way this evening is going, let me guess. It's your apartment."

His laugh was soothing and his eyes creased as the corners wrinkled. She loved the soft effect his amusement had on his handsome face.

"Okay," Preston said. "I guess I set myself up for that one."

They stopped at a quaint coffee shop. When Mia returned from the restroom and joined Preston at a table in a dark corner, a server walked up with two large mugs of steaming champurrado. After thanking her, she took a big sip, hoping the warm drink would help knock the chill off her.

The rich chocolate was flavored with hearty cinnamon. "Wow, this is delicious. I can't believe you found a spot that makes these."

Preston smiled. "I'm glad you like it. I figured you could use something warm and tasty after standing out in that cold garage for who knows how long. Plus, I like the holiday decor and music here."

Mia nodded and bit into the crème-filled pirouette wafer that was dipped into a fluffy cloud of whipped cream for garnish. "This is perfect. And you should see the bathroom. It smells like the North Pole exploded in there."

After a thoughtful pause, he concluded, "I'm not sure if that's good or bad." He studied her for a few moments, then asked, "So, are you Mexicana?"

Mia smiled and nodded. "Sí. And a quarter Black on my father's side."

Preston grinned, seeming proud of himself for guessing that she was Mexican. "¿Hablas español?" (Do you speak Spanish?)

"Un poco. ¿Y tú?" (A little. You?)

After Mia confirmed that she spoke a little Spanish, Preston continued. "Sí, hablo español con fluidez. Mi madre es cubana y mi padre es afrodescendiente." (Yes, I speak Spanish fluently. My mother is Cuban and my father is Black)

"Ahh, Cubano. That definitely would have been my guess. Do you speak Spanish at home?"

"Yeah, my mom and I switch back and forth." She noticed the warmth in his eyes at the mention of his mom and assumed they were close. He continued. "And most of my extended family only speaks Spanish."

Mia nodded thoughtfully. She was comfortable with the brief moments of silence that passed between them. Most of the guys she knew spent the entire time talking about themselves. She appreciated his effort to get to know her better.

After a few moments, Preston asked, "So, are you going to confirm or deny my initial suspicion?"

Mia lifted a brow. "Huh? What are you suspicious about? You don't even know me."

Preston chuckled, clearly amused by her reaction. "I like a little spice, for real."

Mia was surprised by how something as simple as hearing his laughter could instantly begin lifting her spirits.

"Before we went inside the auto parts store, I guessed that you're a fashion designer or a mixed media artist. But you never corrected me so...?" In the well-lit coffee shop, she suddenly noticed how thick his eyebrows were as they kept inching further up his forehead. Like two fuzzy little wooly bear caterpillars. Just adorable. She pressed the tips of her acrylics into her palms, fighting the urge to extend her thumb and smooth them. Instead, she reached for her mug and hid her smile behind a slow, sweet sip.

After making him wait for almost a full minute, she said, "Well, that's interesting. But nah. I'm a commercial interior architect."

Preston nodded, crossing his arms and slightly leaning back in his chair. "So, you know what this entrepreneur life's about. Straight up taxing."

"You ain't neva lied," she scoffed, polishing off her wafer.

He continued. "It's nice to chop it with someone who understands it for once. Today was a tough day for me, too."

Mia frowned. "Sorry to hear that. Was I your last customer of the evening?"

"Nah. But once I determined your battery was shot, I decided to call it a wrap and leave the towing to my team for the rest of the night."

"Well, don't let me cost you a bag by sitting here sipping cocoa over chasing those contracts. I'm sure nights like these are busy for you and we can all use extra money around the holidays."

Preston waved a hand. "Oh, nah...nah. Don't even worry about that. It's way too cold to be out there tonight, anyway."

"Well, thank you for bringing me here. I know you're probably short on drivers and juggling a million and one things right now."

"How do you know I don't drive on a regular basis?"

"There's no way. First of all, your Timbs don't have a single mark on them. Second, I looked up your company while I was waiting for you to arrive and you have over three hundred customer reviews. That's far too much business for you to be the only one out there driving. You're probably negotiating new contracts each month."

Preston rubbed his chin, his eyes scanning the wall before returning to Mia.

She sighed. "Okay, if I'm being real, I was pulling you up to leave a bad review. You were very late, and I did end up losing a potential client tonight. But I changed my mind when I saw all the great things people had to say about A. Gómez Towing. I decided to wait until after we conducted business to provide feedback."

"I can understand why you would initially want to leave a bad review and I apologize again for your missed appointment," he said. "Hopefully, we haven't ruined our chances of making you a happy customer."

She shook her head. "Not necessary. I'm just giving you a hard time."

He smirked. "On the other hand, you're saying my undeniable charm saved me tonight from those raging Twitter fingers?"

"That's *not* what I'm saying. I just believe in giving grace - especially as a fellow small business owner."

"Well, I can appreciate that. It would have been nice if your potential client could have extended you the same grace."

"Agreed," she said, shrugging. "But I guess the project wasn't meant for me."

They sat in thoughtful silence for a few moments before Mia added, "Another reason I didn't leave a bad review was I didn't want to be included in those five percent of obnoxious and rude people who left you bad reviews."

"That's part of this business. We don't get to interact with people at their best moments," he rubbed his chin. "So, tell me about your commercial interior architecture business. Did I say that right?"

"You did."

"Alright, so I'm a potential investor. Give me your pitch."

Mia looked around. "Right now? In the middle of a coffee shop?"

"If I've learned anything over the past several years as an entrepreneur, it's that fortune favors the bold."

Mia stared at Preston, who was still leaning back in his chair with his arms crossed. His face held an open challenge as if he were thinking, *Go on, sell me this pen.*

"Well," Mia shrugged and took another sip of her lukewarm beverage. "I need clients. So, I guess now's as good a time as any for practicing my elevator pitch."

He nodded at her, waiting patiently for her to begin.

She cleared her throat. "Here goes nothing."

Mia stood and brushed down the front of her skirt. Preston sat up straighter in his seat, his eyes widening as he looked around the small café. But she was already launching into her spiel.

"Good evening, everyone. I'm Mia Reyes, founder of The Harmony and Heritage Studio. As an interior architect of Black and Mexican descent, my heritage and fashion-forward perspective shapes my bold, eclectic bohemian style. I specialize in designing spaces that reflect your culture, brand, or family's personality. Together, we'll bring your vision to life and create an environment that represents your individuality. Let's create a space that tells your unique story. The Harmony and Heritage Studio—infusing life and legacy into your venue."

As Mia quickly reclaimed her seat, the only sound was the sultry serenade of "My Favorite Things" by Ari Lennox. When she finally looked up from staring at her hands, which were slick with sweat and clenched in her lap, she realized the patrons of the small shop were cheering. High-pitched whistles could be heard in the front corner, along with a chorus of shouts, including "Go off, sis!" "I'd hire you!" and "Don't they have a bulletin board for that?"

"How'd I do?" Mia asked, widening her eyes in anticipation while trying her hardest not to smile.

"Well...very well. Good job," Preston said, nodding feverishly. "That was unexpected and...ballsy."

"Fortune favors the bold, right?"

"Indeed. Have you ever heard the saying, 'The only difference between you and me is that I have a camera on me?'"

Mia nodded. "Yeah, that's a Daymond John quote."

He stared at her for a moment before asking, "You like Daymond John?"

"Of course, who doesn't? A, he's from Brooklyn, B, outside of college, he's single-handedly taught me everything I know about running a business."

When he didn't respond, Mia shrugged. "Anyway, I've been posting my portfolio on a whole bunch of freelance sites without much luck. I specialize in optimizing small spaces, so coming back to Brooklyn has been ideal for me. I enjoy making a small business space feel like a wide-open loft so people feel proud about their little piece of New York."

"You mentioned families in your subway performance. So, you also take on residential clients?"

She shot him a playful glare. "You'd be hard-pressed to find a pitch of that quality on a subway car. But, yeah, I'll take on domestic designs when I'm between commercial clients. Hell, I can't even be picky—I have zero clients right now."

Preston nodded. "Well, I know a few people who may be interested in working with you. I'll pass on their info."

"Much appreciated."

"As far as your commercial services, if I showed you a few pictures of my office space, would you consider redesigning it? I'll share it with my partner and a few staff members. It's pretty cramped."

Mia paused, thinking of a small, musty back office with paperwork piled to the ceiling.

He chuckled. "Did I just catch a nose wrinkle?"

"Well...yeah. Redesigning a tow truck office wasn't exactly on my vision board during design school. But after all you've done to distract me from the events of this shitty night, the least I can do is take a look at it." She noticed the excitement in his eyes and realized she may have already bitten off more than she could chew. "But I'd prefer to see the space in person."

"Great! How's tomorrow? I can have my office manager tune up your car while you're there. He's also a part-time mechanic."

Mia chewed her bottom lip, weighing the chance to land a new client while finally fixing her car's long-standing issues in one afternoon. "This offer's getting more tempting by the minute. Tell me more about your project goals on the way back to my car."

Chapter Three

The next day, Mia had just left her parent's house and was pulling up to a red light when her phone buzzed. When she identified the caller, she froze. It was her apartment leasing office again. Her rent was now two weeks late, and she was no closer to making a payment than when they called a few days ago. With no active clients, she was hesitant to accept the call, but she knew it was time to face the music.

"Hi, Traci. How are you today?"

"I'm doing good, Mia. I hope you're also well. I was just ringing you to let you know that your account has officially been marked as past due for the balance on your account. Would you like to make your rent payment over the phone today?"

Mia released a slow breath, her fingers tightening around the steering wheel. "I'm actually about to walk into a prospective client meeting as we speak. If all goes well, I plan to provide them with a proposal and request a deposit today. I would just need a little time for the check to clear."

There was a brief pause. "So, you're saying you'll be able to bring your account up to a current status before the end of the week?"

The hint of disbelief in Traci's words lurked beneath the veneer of her professional tone. Mia knew she was on thin ice. Feeling the weighty words she didn't fully believe, she said, "That's the plan."

"Okay, I'll make a note on your account. However, I want to be clear: if we don't hear from you by close of business on Friday, we'll have no choice but to file a tenant's termination for nonpayment. That will also impact Arden, as you're both listed on the lease agreement, even though she's already made her half of the rent payment."

A sinking feeling pooled in her stomach. "I'm crystal clear. Thanks for your call, Traci."

The urge to scream bubbled inside her. *How had everything spiraled so fast?* Just six months ago, her business in Miami was thriving with a full waiting of clients. She knew she was one of the coldest young designers in the region. When she first decided to return to Brooklyn, one of her Miami clients eagerly offered to cover her travel expenses just to ensure she remained on his dream team for designing his national cluster of vacation rental homes. Now her pipeline was gone and she and her sister were at risk of being evicted from their place. She was thankful to be closer to home with the option of moving back in with her family, but her independence meant everything to her.

It was moments like these, in which she was pushing against expectations and proving her worth, that reminded her that she wasn't just doing this to make a living—she was doing this to finally put to rest the voices that doubted her. The ones that told her, even back when she started in Miami, that she'd be better off playing it safe, settling for less.

Her family meant well, but that had never made their lack of faith in her hurt any less. And she needed to get past it—to validate herself through action, through her own success—because no one else would do it for her. She'd convinced her older sister, Arden, to move in with her to help her cover the rent. The last thing she wanted was to be responsible for getting them both evicted from their first apartment because she couldn't manage her share. All she needed was something to tide herself over until her next big break. She could take it from there.

She spotted an open street parking space and slipped into it. After people-watching for five full minutes, she made the call she'd been putting off for weeks. Desperate times called for desperate measures. The phone rang three times, and just as she was ready to hang up, his voice cut through – flat, with that familiar tinge of boredom.

"Hello."

She closed her eyes for a second to still her voice before she spoke. "Hey, JoJo. How are you?"

"Mia, what's going on?"

"I'm back in Brooklyn," she sang. "So, what's been going on with you? Catch me up."

"Catch you up?"

"Yeah, what's been going on with you? How's your family doing?"

JoJo scoffed. "Mia, we both know you never call just to 'catch up.' Only when you need something, so just tell me what it is."

Taken aback by his clipped tone, Mia took a steadying breath. "Well, I'm sorry you feel that way. I don't want you to think I'm using you. I really appreciate your support, and you've always been there for me when I'm having a hard time."

"Mmm-hmm," he replied, his voice sounding disinterested.

She shifted nervously in her seat. "The truth is, I've been

back for a little over five months now and I have my own place. I lost most of my local client prospects to competitors while I was in Miami, and now I'm working hard to rebuild my local portfolio. I want to exhaust all my options before giving up on my dream. Anyway, a potential client deal just fell through and now my rent is almost a month late."

"How much, Mia?" Mia could hear the irritation in his voice, likely due to her rambling.

"Twelve hundred should do it. I can have it back to you within thirty days."

"No problem. I'll cash app you today."

She exhaled a long breath. "Thanks, JoJo."

"Uh-uh. Now, what's in it for me?"

"If I don't have any money, what else do you think I can offer you?"

His voice dropped. "Let me come see your fine ass."

Mia squeezed her eyes shut and stifled a low groan.

"You seeing someone?" he asked her.

She swallowed back the word 'no' so fast she almost choked on it. That was none of his business. "Aren't you? I heard you're in a relationship now."

"We're not talking about me. Besides, you weren't concerned about her when you were just asking for a favor, were you?"

"JoJo, we've been over this. We broke up more than four years ago. I'm not interested in revisiting that. I appreciate you helping me, but let's be clear—this is just a loan, nothing more. If that's not something you can agree to, I'm going to end this call."

"So, I'm good enough for you to take my money, but not to spend your time with. Am I getting that right?"

Mia shook her head, the words drying up in her throat. She refused to take his bait any longer.

"I guess I have my answer."

"Bet." She had already pulled the phone from her ear and was about to hang up when she heard his voice again.

"Nah, that's fine. I'll let it go this time, but I'm gonna get my date. It's only a matter of time before you'll be calling again and Daddy Jo'll be patiently waiting," he chuckled.

Mia cringed as she hung up and tossed the phone onto the passenger seat. It bounced off and thudded on the floor. Moments later, the familiar cash register sound chimed, signaling the money was transferred to her account. Though it was a relief to know that she and her sister were saved from getting evicted over the next thirty days, she was consumed by the feeling of being bought. It felt like JoJo always found a way to use her financial vulnerability against her, turning his short-term loans into unbearable stress that felt like a claim on her life. This was exactly why she avoided asking him for help.

Even with their rent covered, she still had to figure out how to make enough money to buy Christmas presents. Before finding career success in Miami, she had always shown up at her parents' house empty-handed during the holidays, year after year. Now that her niece and nephew were here, she swore never to give off 'broke auntie' vibes. Over her dead body. She leaned her head back on the seat, as "Oh Santa!" by Mariah Carey played on the radio, a bittersweet soundtrack to her thoughts.

Santa, if you get this letter, won't you help me out?

Where was her Santa right about now? With all the issues piling up, it barely felt like the holiday season. Emotionally drained, Mia scanned the empty street before reclining her seat all the way back. The only thing that might offer her any sense of relief right now was a good, hard cry—without the probing eyes of an audience.

Chapter Four

With a dried face and freshened makeup, Mia pulled up to A. Gómez Towing a couple of hours later. It was early afternoon and a soft dusting of snow glittered under the glow of sunlight. She walked up the gravel driveway and passed the tow truck she'd ridden in with Preston the day before. A small smile tugged at her lips as she remembered his broad shoulders cloaked in a short pea coat. With her mind a million miles away, she approached the heart of the yard. She scanned the property, taking in his setup while trying to gauge the size of his office. The lights were on inside, but it was so quiet she wasn't sure if they were still open. She pulled open the glass door of the small trailer and triggered the door chime, announcing her arrival. A few moments later, a short, jovial-looking man with sandy brown hair emerged from a back room.

"Hello, ma'am. How can I help you today?"

"Hi, I'm Mia Reyes. I'm here to meet with Preston."

His green eyes lit up and his warm smile deepened. "Oh, Mia! Nice to meet you! I'm Trevor, the office manager. Would you like anything to drink? Water, coffee, hot cocoa?"

She could have sworn she caught a glimmer in his eyes when he mentioned the last beverage.

"Water's fine. Thank you, Trevor."

He handed her a chilled bottle from the mini-fridge. "Come with me. Preston's in his office finishing up a few things, but he'll meet you in the conference room shortly."

Mia followed Trevor further into the building and down a narrow hallway. She was pleasantly surprised that the space had more depth than she expected. They passed two offices before entering the conference room. She blinked. The room was dark but every detail felt meticulously arranged. But why? Cushions and a cozy blanket were on a makeshift seating area in the center of the room. Soft piano music played in the background and vases of fresh, colorful bouquets were strategically placed around the room.

"What's all this," she murmured, walking over to sniff a bouquet of red and white orchids.

Mystified, she spun on her heel to take in the ambiance. Her gaze moved from the flowers to the warm, twinkling fairy lights hanging overhead. They cast a glow that danced on the walls.

Trevor nodded with a smile as Mia wandered toward a cluster of balloons in the corner of the room. Small envelopes were attached to each of their strings.

"Those are from Preston," Trevor said. "He'll just be a few more moments. Do you mind if I grab your car keys so I can run it over to my garage for a quick diagnostic?"

"Sure," she said, handing over the keys. "Thanks again for doing this."

"No problem. I'll be back soon," he said and left the room.

She pulled an envelope from one of the balloons. She was surprised by the neat penmanship. *Sorry I 'towed' the line of unprofessionalism last night! I promise not to be fashionably late to any more of our meetings.*

Mia shook her head, feeling her cheeks burn with second-hand embarrassment. She appreciated good wordplay, but this wasn't it. "Fashionably late indeed. Boy cost me a bag."

Someone joined in her laughter and she turned to face Preston, who was walking into the room. He wore a cable-knit navy blue sweater with dark jeans and hard bottoms. His features softened with relief. "I'm glad you found that funny. I asked Trevor to help me write a few of them."

"Whew! I hope this one didn't come from you," she said, holding up the card.

"Welcome to my humble tow truck office. I hope you don't mind the unconventional setting."

"Thanks. This was...unexpected. What's all this about?"

He smiled, stepping closer. "I wanted to apologize for the inconvenience I caused you last night. I know I disrupted your evening plans, and I wanted to show you how much I respect your time."

She nodded. "Well, this is definitely unique. I don't think I've ever found a tow truck office so...romantic?"

He motioned toward the blanket and pillows. "Please, have a seat. I got you a little something." He gestured toward a small table where a cup of hot cocoa awaited her.

"How sweet." He handed her the mug and she took a tepid sip.

As she settled onto the cushions, he joined her. "Thanks for coming by."

"My pleasure. Especially when it's for something like this," she said, subtly filling her lungs with the silky cedarwood scent of his office.

"So..." Preston said, rubbing his hands together.

"So–" Mia started.

We're awkward as shit, she thought, glancing down to

study her thigh-high boots as blood rushed to her cheeks. "Please. Go ahead."

"Like I said, I got you something."

"Oh, it wasn't the cocoa."

He handed her a wrapped box. "Open it. I promise it's not another battery."

"So that *was* your note. Trying to blame all that corniness on my boy Trevor," Mia joked as she carefully unwrapped the box and pulled back the tissue paper. She gasped. "Preston, this is gorgeous." She held up an elegant ornament with her company's logo. "How did you get this made so fast?"

"A good friend owns a Christmas-themed Etsy store. Apparently, people buy this kind of stuff year-round."

"Thank you. I can't wait to hang this on my tree. Once I get one..."

They shared a smile.

He licked his lips and she watched them glisten until he spoke, "About last night...are you going to read the rest of your notes?"

She nodded, trying to clear her thoughts as he got up to bring the balloon bouquet over to her. As she read through the notes that continued making light of their encounter, they laughed and joked. By the time she finished reading the last one, she was almost disappointed that it was over. "Thank you," she said, genuinely touched. "I appreciate the effort you put into making things right."

He nodded, holding her gaze. "I'm serious about us working together on transforming this tow truck office into something I can be proud of."

She smiled, reluctant to break up their cozy moment, but they had work to do. She was eager to learn what it would be like to partner with him on this project. "Yes! I have a few ideas already. But first, I need the grand tour."

"You got it."

He stood, then extended his hand to help her up. She placed her palm in his hand, which completely swallowed hers. Once on her feet, she scanned the room again as he unplugged the fairy lights and turned on the overhead lights. She blinked against the brightness and took in the cool mint green wall, which was decorated with three-piece canvas abstract art. A column of wall-to-ceiling windows were framed with chevron drapes, allowing plenty of sunshine to stream in. Lined against the walls were two large mahogany desks along with bookshelves holding ceramic vases and hand-molded artistic pieces. She assumed the conference table and chairs had been moved elsewhere. The carpet was clean but outdated and the ceiling fan was an eyesore, but the contemporary space still surpassed her expectations.

"So this, of course, is our conference room, where we host our current and potential clients."

Mia followed Preston to his office. It was a modest space with several bookshelves stocked full of college textbooks, business manuals, and guides, but the first thing to catch her eye was a large framed picture of Daymond John. Her mind flashed back to the quote he'd quizzed her on in the coffee shop. She remembered the way his eyes lit up when she recognized the source. Now, seeing the picture of the mogul in his office, she finally understood the connection.

As she sank into one of his cushioned leather chairs and he sat behind the large cherry oak desk, her eyes continued to roam the room. State licenses and certifications were neatly displayed beside framed motivational quotes, the walls practically buzzing with ambition.

Mia shifted in her seat as something nagged at her. The tidy office seemed almost too perfect, too quiet. "Something struck me as odd as I was walking up to the building," she began, glancing at Preston, who was watching her intently.

"Where are all the towed cars? This is a tow truck company, right?"

She watched as those cuddly little wooly bears on his forehead slowly scrunched together, forming the most adorable thoughtful frown. It made her wonder what was on his mind, but she pressed on, determined to stay on task. "I was expecting to be triggered by seeing an impound lot. Lord knows I've been to more than my fair share of those during my college years."

"You and me both," he said with a chuckle. "But nah, we don't have one of those. We tow vehicles to the location the owner requests. Except when it's impounded due to a DUI, for driving with a suspended license, outstanding warrants....that kind of stuff. We take those to a contracted storage facility."

"So that's how you get your storage fees?"

"No, the vehicle owner or insurance company pays storage fees to the facility directly."

"And you've probably worked out a percentage or flat fee arrangement for what the facility collects," Mia concluded. Then, it was her turn to frown. "But aren't daily storage fees and fines a significant source of revenue for towing companies? You must have a good reason for passing up that type of passive income."

His brow furrowed as he watched her cross her shapely legs.

"Yeah, storage fees are a money generator for some tow companies, but based on the extensive market research we conducted while developing our business plan, we realized the cost and maintenance of an on-site storage facility wouldn't be worth the revenue stream from the storage fees. We found we could generate far more money in towing fees alone if we focused our efforts on developing partnerships with insurance companies, roadside assistance programs, local law enforcement, the city, car dealerships, repair shops, parking garages, private property managers, and fleet management companies. The business we get from those contracts alone is more than we can handle. We had to hire six more drivers just this year. Besides..." He paused just as her eyes were glazing over. "Mia?"

She cleared her throat, saying his name at the same time he said hers. "Preston...I'm so sorry. Please don't hold that against me. I'm still very interested in working with you."

He held up his hand. "It's no problem, really. I know this isn't the most intriguing topic."

She shook her head. "No, it's not that. I just had a long day yesterday. After you changed my battery in the parking garage, I realized I was almost out of gas, so I stopped for some after we parted ways. Once I finally made it back home, I was hungry and had a taste for mallorca. So, my roommate Arden, who is also my sister, and I ended up making a whole breakfast spread. I'm talking fresh squeezed orange juice for mimosas and everything. Then I had to update my portfolio early this morning and draft a preliminary design contract for our meeting. Needless to say, I didn't get very much sleep last night."

A smirk tugged at his lips. He opened his mouth, seemed to think better of it, then gave a small nod instead before smoothly shifting the conversation. "Don't worry about it. As I said, I appreciate you coming out on short notice. So, what questions do you have for me?"

She sat up straighter, flipping to a fresh page in her notebook. "Can you tell me about the functionality of this space? I see a conference room, so I'm assuming administrative tasks, client meetings, and perhaps dispatching?"

He nodded. "All of the above. We have a total of six rooms. The lobby doubles as Trevor's office, my office, and a small back office where Luna, our call center rep, sits. We also have a kitchen, a filing and supply room, and a mother's room."

She looked up from her notebook to find Preston smiling

at her like he understood her shock to hear about something like that at a small tow truck office. "Luna has a four-month-old son. When she returned to work after her maternity leave, I converted the supply room into a private space for her. Once we do an official tour, you can take a look. I'm sure there's plenty more you can do with that space. I'd like to add a meditation corner with yoga mats and a wireless speaker for calming music."

Mia couldn't help asking, "Did Luna ask you to provide the nursing room for her?"

"No. She shouldn't have to. As her employer, it's my responsibility to anticipate her needs."

"Agreed," Mia said, nodding and all but swooning in her chair. She remembered a friend of hers telling her that she had to fight her employer for nearly three months for a quiet space to pump her milk after having her daughter. She had to submit a detailed proposal along with her request. Once it was approved eight months later, she was no longer nursing nor an employee at that fine establishment. Yet, Preston seemed to have empathy and compassion for his employees by ensuring their needs were being met and in a timely manner. She wanted to fan herself, but reached for her bottled water instead. After taking a sip, she said, "That was very thoughtful of you. How many employees use this workspace?"

"Just five of us. Shelley, my business partner, myself, Trevor, Luna, and Darla, our bookkeeper and payroll manager. Darla only comes in occasionally; she often works from home."

Mia nodded. "Good to know. So, when you're not hosting clients, it's pretty quiet around here."

"Right, not a lot of routine traffic. So, what do you think of the place? Honestly."

She looked around. "Honestly? It's not too bad. I really like the soft colors. I may have gone with similar ones, especially since you get such great natural light, and the colors represent your brand. I also noticed your furniture fits your brand aesthetic perfectly. Did you pick it out?"

"Actually, my mom did most of the decor. Shelley and I were on a tight budget when we first acquired this business, so Mom selected and paid for the majority of the furniture and art as our business shower gift. But I'm not sentimentally attached to any of it, so please feel free to change anything you like. This'll all be yours to play with."

"Okay, Mama Gómez! She may be my competition out here in these Brooklyn designer streets."

Preston smiled. She noticed the pride in his eyes and took a mental note. Possible mama's boy? Not necessarily a bad thing. Then her eyes narrowed slightly as the rest of his words sunk in. "And will your partner Shelley share your sentiment about me taking the lead on the office redesign?"

"Shelley's been on me about doing more with this place for years. She wants a more prestigious touch because we plan to work with more corporate clients. So, yes, she's on board and eager to review your proposal."

"That's good because I don't want to step on any toes. Not mama's and especially not your partner's."

A flicker of amusement crossed his face, though she didn't recall saying anything funny.

They reviewed Mia's portfolio and Preston stated his appreciation for her innovative use of color, attention to detail, and signature style. Although her elevator speech at the coffee shop was a bit boastful, she wanted to show him it was on point. Mia mastered revitalizing small spaces and believed she could do a lot with the trailer. She noticed his pleased expression, making her think she'd secured the project. She felt proud of the work she'd shown him. Preston seemed completely at ease, his eyes shining with approval.

They measured the windows and she verified each room's

dimensions on the floor plan. He narrowed his choices down to three paint colors for the lobby and conference room and she helped him select a few furniture pieces from the store's website, where he had a credit line. Once he confirmed his budget, they created a spreadsheet using formulas Mia had created. She promised to bring in local art and carpet samples for him to consider later that week. After a couple of hours, Preston approved her quote and list of initial recommendations, and they each felt satisfied with their progress.

"Let me make a few calls first, but I'm pretty confident we'll be able to wrap this up by the third week of January," Mia said, sticking her attaché case into her messenger bag.

Preston leaned back in his chair, nodding with an approving smile. "That works. With the holidays, I was expecting late February."

"I still have a few contacts from my associate's program."

"That's great," He glanced at the wall clock. "Do you want to join me for a late lunch?

"Oh, Mr. Goméz, one thing you should know about me is, I'll never, ever turn down a meal," Mia said with a playful wink.

Preston chuckled, standing up. "Noted. Let me grab my coat and we can go."

Chapter Five

They devoured Reuben sandwiches at a bodega, savoring the warm, tangy bites that disappeared far too quickly. After lunch, Preston insisted they take a walk, his eyes twinkling as they strolled down the sidewalk, their arms occasionally brushing against each other. The air was crisp, and the sky had that wintry sheen that promised snow. Mia shivered, tugging her coat tighter as she eyed him with curiosity.

"Where are we going?" she asked, narrowing her eyes playfully. Preston's lips curved into a mischievous smile, but he remained tight-lipped. Instead of answering, he reached for her hand. The warmth of his fingers laced with hers sent an unexpected shiver up her spine, and she fought to keep her composure.

A few minutes later, they rounded a corner, and Mia gasped softly. Waiting at the curb was a beautiful horse-drawn carriage, festively adorned with strings of twinkling lights, red bows, and a sprig of mistletoe hanging from the roof. The driver, a jolly older man in a Santa hat, tipped his hat toward them.

Preston turned to Mia, his grin widening at her stunned expression. "Thought we could take the scenic route for a bit. What do you think?"

Mia blinked, her heart swelling at the sight. It was like something out of a holiday movie—the lights, the horse with a red and green plaid blanket draped over its back, and the sound of jingle bells echoing softly from the reins. She smiled, giving his hand a light squeeze. "This is... amazing. But are you sure this isn't... too much?" she asked. She didn't understand why he'd gone to so much trouble when hey were just business associates.

Preston raised an eyebrow, playing it cool. "Just trying to make sure my designer feels inspired. You know, a festive ambiance," he said. His voice was steady, but his eyes told her it was more than just a professional outing.

He helped her up into the carriage, his hand lingering on her waist for a moment longer than necessary. She settled onto the cushioned seat, her heart racing as he climbed in beside her. She let out a giggle and the driver flashed her a smile before signaling the horse to move. The carriage started off at a gentle pace, the clip-clop of hooves providing a soothing rhythm as they began their ride through the decorated streets of Brooklyn.

The neighborhoods were aglow with holiday lights— strings of multicolored bulbs crisscrossing over the streets, wreaths hanging from lampposts, and store windows decked out with holiday displays. People bustled along the sidewalks, bundled in scarves and coats, their faces lit with smiles as they carried shopping bags. Children pointed and laughed, captivated by the festive decorations and the occasional blow-up snowman in front yards.

Mia leaned back, trying her best to relax, to let the warmth and festive ambiance distract her from Preston's close proximity. She turned to look at him, catching his gaze already on her.

A tender softness settled in his eyes, and her stomach fluttered. She cleared her throat, shaking her head with a chuckle. "How did you even arrange this on such short notice?"

Preston shrugged, his smile modest. "You're not the only one with connections around the city. I figured you could use a little holiday magic after yesterday. Plus, I like to think a carriage ride is part of a well-rounded client experience."

The carriage swayed gently, and as Mia shifted to make herself more comfortable, her shoulder brushed against his. She felt the warmth of his arm and instinctively held her breath, the line between professionalism and something else blurring faster than she could blink.

They passed a park where a group of carolers stood near the entrance, their voices rising in harmony as they sang "O Holy Night." The melody filled the air, and Mia's heart swelled, the romance of the moment almost overwhelming. She shivered slightly, and without a word, Preston draped an arm around her shoulders. It was casual, so casual that anyone else might think it was nothing, but to Mia, every nerve in her body lit up at his touch.

She looked up, giving him a questioning glance, her lips parted as if to say something. Preston just smiled, his gaze flicking up to the mistletoe hanging above them. "Looks like we're under some obligations here," he said, his voice teasing but his eyes serious.

Her pulse quickened. This was a line—one that, if crossed, could change everything. A kiss could be an accident, something that just happened in the spirit of the season. But it would also be a declaration that whatever was building between them was real. She was afraid to cross it, yet she found herself leaning closer, holding his gaze. Should she let him kiss her on the cheek?

She cleared her throat, forcing a grin. "I don't think mistletoe counts in a work setting," she joked, trying to diffuse the moment, but her voice came out weaker than she'd intended.

Preston's smile softened. He dipped his head slightly, enough that their foreheads almost touched. "You're probably right," he whispered, his breath warm against her skin. "But you can't blame a guy for trying."

The space between them disappeared for a breath, a heartbeat, a moment that seemed to stretch into forever. And then, as if the universe couldn't help itself, the carriage hit a small bump, jolting them just enough that Mia fell against him, her face ending up inches from his.

She blinked, and there it was—that undeniable electricity surging between them. Her hand splayed across his chest, and she could feel his heart pounding just as hard as hers. Preston swallowed, his gaze flicking from her eyes to her lips, then back again. They were so close that she could feel the sexual tension radiating off of him. The thick anticipation made her pulse race.

The driver cleared his throat, oblivious to the silent exchange between them. "Nice night for a ride, huh?" he said cheerily.

Mia pulled back, her cheeks flushed. She quickly adjusted herself, smoothing out her coat. Preston exhaled a slow breath, nodding to the driver with a tight smile. "Yeah, it is," Preston replied.

Mia dared a glance at Preston, and their eyes met. His lips twitched in a smug smile that seemed to promise that this wasn't over, not by a long shot.

"Are you two from Brooklyn?" the driver asked after a few moments.

"Yes, we both are," he answered for them.

"Nice. Well, I hope you can take another ride with us soon. Please tell a friend."

"I'll do you one better," Mia said, pulling out her phone. "I'll give you a five-star rating."

Out of the corner of her eye, she saw Preston shift in order to face her. "Oh, really?"

Fighting off laughter, she said, "Yup."

"So he gets his five-star before AGT?" he asked in mock disappointment.

"Well, what can I say?" Mia shrugged. "The man was prompt. That's an automatic five-star right there."

They pulled up to the end of the ride laughing. The driver tipped his hat and wished them a Merry Christmas. Preston tucked a couple of twenties into his tip jar before exiting and extending a hand to help Mia down. Their joined gloved hands felt natural, so she allowed their connection to linger.

She squeezed his hand. "Thank you for this," she finally said, her voice softer. "It was a really fun way to experience the holidays in my city once again."

Preston smiled, nodding. "Anytime, Mia. And hey, maybe one day, we can do something like this without a work excuse."

She fought to keep her expression steady, though her breathing was quickening by the second. "Yeah, maybe," she said, allowing her lips to curve into a smile. And with that, they walked side by side with Mia knowing that whatever this was between them, it was just getting started.

***

They stopped for white chocolate caramel milkshakes that really hit the spot, even with the biting winter air swirling around them.

"This milkshake's hittin.' Thanks for introducing me to Mia's Brooklyn bakery, although I think you're a little biased." Preston shot her a playful side-eye.

"Yeah, her name's dope, but these shakes speak for themselves."

"No lie," he laughed as she slurped loudly, then smacked her lips. He watched her, noticing the stark contrast between her current casual demeanor and her polished professional side he'd seen before. While he admired her focus and knack for offering equitable solutions, he was equally drawn to her relaxed sense of humor. "But we look like two fools walking around drinking milkshakes in the dead of winter."

"As good as this shake is, I don't give a damn what I look like right now."

"Let's give your feet a rest," Preston gestured toward her knee-high boots and led them toward a bench. They brushed off the snow before sitting down.

"Whooo!" Mia squealed. She wiggled like a chill shot up her spine. She set down her shake and blew on her gloved hands. "I haven't been outside in the winter for this long in a while. Okay, you may have had a point earlier about the poorly timed milkshakes."

"Come here," Preston held out his arm.

She hesitated only for a moment before snuggling into his side, her eyes gently closing as she seemed to relax against him. She took a deep breath, her nose brushing his arm, and he wondered why she was sniffing him like that. When he caught a smile on her face, he figured she appreciated his holiday cologne. It had undertones of spices, vanilla, and musk. She looked so peaceful and there was something about the way she was curling up against him—a near stranger—that surprised him. The carriage was one thing, but on a public park bench? A fleeting thought crossed his mind: she had to be feeling the same type of connection that he had. Something had been slowly building between them all evening.

"You good," he asked, feeling her squirm.

"All good."

"Still culture shocked? You're a long way from Miami."

"Boy, please. I'm fine. I could do BK winters in my sleep. Just need to get readjusted, that's all."

"Aww, there's that accent I've been looking for. It's about time. Act like it, then."

He laughed as she slugged him in his chest.

After a moment, she asked, "Should I be nervous about being booed up out here in public with you like this? I mean, you're scheduling horse-drawn carriages and shit. I don't want to get my front tooth knocked out by a random ex hurling rock snowballs or whatever."

Preston stared at her, dumbfounded at her random question. "What?"

Mia shrugged. "I'm just saying..."

She didn't move a muscle and he realized she was patiently waiting for his response. "No vengeful exes to worry about."

"Or jump-offs? Groupies?"

"None of the above. I've been so focused on growing the business that it seems like all I have time for is working, eating, and sleeping," he said.

He felt a slight squeeze on his bicep. "And it seems like you've found time to exercise."

He raised a brow, glad she couldn't see his broad smile. Her touch felt good. "I have. But I haven't found a woman who intrigues me enough to want to invest the little bit of free time and energy I have into starting a relationship. If I meet a girl and it leads to something, we do what we do and part ways amicably. No drama involved."

"So what characteristics are worthy of investing your time?" She asked, leaning back to get a good look at him.

"A woman with a clear vision of what she wants. A team player who understands give and take, knowing that no relationship is going to be perfect, but the more you put into it, the more you'll get out of it. Someone who knows who she is but doesn't take herself too seriously. She can laugh at herself and learn from her mistakes."

"Mmm-hmm," she murmured, before nestling back into his side.

"What about you?"

"Ditto."

They spent a few minutes lost in their individual thoughts. Then Preston squeezed her hand gently. She laced her fingers between his and snaked her other arm tight around his waist. The snow flurries spun in gentle circles around them, glowing against the night sky. The snow-covered street casted an almost dreamlike peace over the scene.

When she gazed up at him, he wondered if she'd noticed the majestic landscape before them. His eyes softened as they fixed on her. He began closing in on slowly.

Are we doing this? We're doing this, he thought.

She lifted her chin and parted her lips, and he let his mind relax. When her eyes fluttered closed, he pressed his lips against hers. The cool chocolate taste of her lips was soft and sinfully sweet. He pulled back and placed another kiss on her lips while softly massaging her palm with his fingertips. As he pressed into her skin, the chill of the evening air eased away. He deepened their kiss, elevating their combined heat. It was enough to melt the drifting snowflakes as he completely forgot where he was. He swirled his tongue around hers and she moaned softly. He felt her gently palm the back of his head. His insides warmed and he felt her snuggle further into their embrace. It was easy, innocent, and natural. After a few moments, he felt a gentle squeeze from her hand. He eased away, breaking their kiss. When she gazed up at him, her smile mirrored his. He helped her up before they gathered their shakes and walked back to the train stop hand-in-hand.

* * *

On the train, a quiet sense of contentment settled between them as each of them were lost in their thoughts. As they drew closer to the office, reality began to settle in. The stretched silence grew uncomfortable, and Mia began to feel awkward. They had shared an incredible moment, but they were at the beginning of their professional relationship and she was unsure how they should move forward.

She cleared her throat, looking up at him with a tentative smile. "So, um, this is new territory for us."

Preston returned her smile. "Yeah, it is."

"I enjoyed our evening together and I enjoyed that kiss even more. But I don't want things to be weird between us."

He nodded, his lips forming a gentle smile. "I've been thinking about that too. We'll be working closely together over the next few weeks... and I don't want to mess things up. But I also don't want to ignore what's happening here." He squeezed her hand gently, as if emphasizing the connection between them.

Mia nodded, glancing down at their joined hands. "Right. It's gotten... complicated. But we're both grown enough to handle it. We just need to communicate. I don't want to jeopardize our professional relationship either, but I like this... I want to see where this goes." She looked up, her eyes meeting his. There was warmth there, but she also sensed vulnerability.

Preston let out a breath, nodding. "Yeah, I like this too. It feels easy." He paused, then added, "What if we just... take it slow? No pressure. We keep our work stuff separate and give each other space to figure this out?"

Mia's shoulders relaxed. "I think that's a good idea. We don't need to rush anything." She gave his hand a little squeeze as they pulled up to their stop. "And, just so we're on the same page... I'm not seeing anyone else." Her cheeks flushed slightly as they stepped off the train. But once they reached the platform, she kept her gaze steady on his.

His lips parted in a grin as relief washed over his face. "I'm not seeing anyone either." The train rushed by them and he reached up, tucking a loose strand of hair away from her face. "I'm glad we're talking about this. I don't want anything to be left unsaid."

As Preston's lips moved against hers earlier, warmth enveloped her body, but her heart hesitated. Could she let herself believe that this time, things would be different? Trusting others had often led to pain, and yet, there she was—hoping and wanting a different outcome. When she let her body melt into his, she'd promised herself that she would try, just this once, to let herself trust the process.

Mia nodded, her heart pounding in her chest as she felt a strange mix of excitement and relief. "Most definitely. Life's too short for bullshitting. Let's just be straightforward with each other."

Preston brought her hand to his lips, pressing a soft kiss to her knuckles. "Always."

They climbed the stairs and as they walked out to the street, the streetlights glowed against the evening sky. They walked toward A. Goméz Towing with their hands still entwined.

"I'm really glad I met you, Mia," Preston said. "Whatever happens, I'm grateful for this... for us."

"So am I. More than you know."

"Hey, I was thinking," Preston said, "how long are you going to hold out on that five-star review for A. Goméz Towing?"

She laughed. "What kind of operation are you running, boy? You can't Deebo customers into giving you five-star reviews."

"Deebo," he feigned shock and innocence as those wooly bears danced on his forehead. "Never that. Just a friendly reminder, Ms. Reyes."

As their laughter faded, they fell into a comfortable silence and walked the rest of the way with their arms intertwined.

* * *

It had been only a couple of days since the park, and Preston had already sent Mia a couple of client referrals. She was grateful for his vote of confidence in her and thanked him. They both wanted quotes, but she assured Preston that she wouldn't be taking them on until after they reached AGT's key project milestones. She didn't want to lose focus or traction, and providing the meditation room was too important to Preston to rush through it. She knew it wasn't essential that they scout for furniture and accessories together, but she suspected he was using this appointment as an excuse to spend more time with her. Truth be told, she didn't mind his company at all. It wasn't often that she had a client so genuinely invested in the energy and feel of every inch of their space, and she enjoyed every minute of their time together.

"How about this one?" Preston called, standing by a deep emerald-green velvet armchair, one hand draped casually over the back.

Mia approached, tilting her head while considering it. She brushed her fingers against the soft fabric, her eyes lifting to meet his. "I think it's perfect. The color works for the room, especially with the natural wood elements we're adding."

Preston grinned, his gaze lingering on her for just a second longer than usual. Her stomach fluttered, doing that same little dance it did whenever Preston was around—a mix of excitement, anticipation, and the pressing desire to be near him. They'd been spending more time together lately—on the phone and in person—and it felt... easy. Comfortable. And it scared her a little.

"We make an excellent team," Preston said, giving her a

quick wink. He looked genuinely happy, standing there in the middle of a furniture shop, discussing fabric colors and décor for a room that would be used mostly by women. Mia allowed herself to mirror his smile.

"Excuse me," came a gentle voice. They both turned to see a woman in her late fifties, with long, gray-streaked hair tied back loosely, holding a tray with polished crystals. "I overheard you discussing a meditation room. You might be interested in these. They're perfect for creating positive energy."

Mia stepped closer, intrigued. The collection of crystals were stunning—amethyst, rose quartz, citrine, all neatly arranged. "These are beautiful," she said, reaching out to touch the smooth surface of an amethyst.

The woman smiled with warm eyes. "You seem like such a lovely couple—you exude dynamic energy. I think any of these would be perfect for the space you're creating together."

Mia froze, her eyes darting to Preston's. He was looking at her with an eyebrow raised and an amused smile playing at his lips. Warmth rushed into her cheeks and she quickly looked back at the woman, forcing a polite smile. "Oh, we're not..." she started, but the words caught in her throat.

"Thanks for your kind words, but we're just collaborating on a work project together," Preston finished for her, but she noticed his tone was light and almost playful.

The woman nodded knowingly, her smile never faltering. "Of course, of course. Well, even so, these crystals are wonderful for creating a peaceful and balanced atmosphere."

She handed Mia a rose quartz, leaning in and speaking softly, "This one's for love and harmony, sweetheart. It's always good to have around."

Mia gasped. The weight of the crystal in her palm, along with the shimmer in the woman's eyes was too much for her. She stole a glance at Preston who gave her a soft smile, his gaze warm and pure. For a moment, the world seemed to close in on just the two of them, standing in the middle of a spiritual living store, her holding a rose quartz meant for love.

"We'll take it," Preston said, his voice invading her thoughts.

Mia nodded. "Yes, thanks for your help."

As they continued browsing the shop, the rose quartz tucked safely into Mia's bag, she stole a few glances at Preston. The shop owner's words echoed in her mind—"you both seem like such a lovely couple." And for the first time in a long time, Mia let herself wonder—what if? What if they weren't just colleagues or collaborators? What if there was something more between them, waiting to be discovered?

She shook the thought away, but the underlying warmth lingered. She smiled like a teenager as Preston cracked a joke about the overwhelming scent of sage coming from the corner of the shop. He was thoughtful, giving, and caring. She felt good whenever she was around him. Maybe... just maybe this could be something real. Maybe it already was.

Chapter Six

The next week, Preston stepped off the train and walked the few blocks to the gym. He held the door for a group of older women decked out from head to toe in neon colors. He smiled, admiring the pep in their step and how innocent they looked. That was until each of them complimented his looks and the last one pointed out his "flawless buns of steel" to the group.

"Hey, Prez." He heard his name sung like a sweet song. He looked up to see a pair of glossy lips pulled into a flirty smile.

"Hey there," he said with a slight nod.

"You left your key fob in the locker room last time." The keychain dangled from her long pointy fingernail covered in sparkling gold crystals.

He double-checked his key ring, then groaned inwardly as he walked over to the counter to retrieve his gym fob from the young woman. Drinking him in by the eyeful and leaning against the glass counter of the product display case, the woman's full-C breasts eagerly tested the limitations of her polo shirt's thin material. As Preston gingerly slid the fob off her nail, she dragged her tongue over her lower lip. He mumbled his gratitude, averting his eyes toward the overhead banner of the entryway that read, "Welcome to a stronger, healthier you. Your journey starts here."

"Oh, you're more than welcome, Prez. Anything for you," she said, giving him a flirty finger wave.

Once he made it safely to the locker room, after periodically looking over his shoulder, he let out a long sigh of relief. Ivy had been sweating him hard since the first day he'd signed up at the gym. No matter what day or time he came, she was always there, ready to greet him with that same dubious smile. She couldn't have been more than nineteen years old; even worse, she was the little sister of one of his closest friends. There wasn't a chance in hell he would ever consider giving her a second look. But that didn't stop her from giving it her best shot every time.

With Bad Bunny blasting in his ear pods, he sat on the bench and changed into his basketball shorts, sleeveless tee, and sneakers. He leaned back and averted his eyes when a teenager strolled past him fully nude and proud as a peacock. *Hell's going on here?* He shook his head, reaching into his bag for his bandages. While bent over, wrapping his right knee, he heard a voice call out, "Bay bro! I got one question for you. Are you ready for this ass whoopin'?"

Preston smiled instantly, looking up to see Lennox sliding his gym bag off his shoulder. He stood and they exchanged daps. "What's good, big bro? Already on the bullshit, I see."

"Nah, it's all fun and games..." Lennox chuckled, taking a quick swig from his water bottle. "'Til I start playing for real."

Preston shook his head. "Whatever, man. How long you in town for?"

"A week and a half. Trying to close this deal."

"I hope it works out for you, bro," Preston said.

"Thanks, man. I just left Halo's office. My mom needed help moving some hair products to her beauty supply store.

She didn't want them delivered directly there because she's worried about the neighborhood. A few weeks ago, a delivery driver left a package on the stoop of her store after hours, and it got stolen. It took weeks before they agreed to issue a refund."

"I swear, parents think we're just sitting around with nothing to do," Preston shook his head. "Dad still has that office with all that money he has saved up? When's he gonna retire?"

"Who knows? He claims his best working years are still ahead of him."

Shrugging, Preston stretched one leg on the bench. "Enough about that dude. How's the love life?"

"Slow motion."

Preston lifted a brow. "That's all you got to say? 'Slow motion?'"

Lennox shrugged, slipping on his sneakers. "Pretty much. Been working long hours, so dating's not a priority right now."

"I respect that. Business is great right now. I gotta force myself to log off and go to sleep."

"Right. We definitely got that workaholic gene from Dad."

"Fa sho."

Lennox smirked. "Enough with the small talk. You ready to catch this heat on the court?"

"Man, what you talkin' 'bout? I stay ready."

After Preston served his older brother a piping-hot ass whooping on a shiny platter, they grabbed a few slices at a corner pizzeria. They sat at a counter facing the street, watching people stroll by the vintage shops, boutiques, and farmers' markets.

"So, she left Brooklyn for an interior design internship in

Miami?" Lennox asked, sprinkling red pepper flakes on his slice.

"Yeah, post-grad. They offered her a position, but she didn't want to live that far from family long-term. She worked with a few clients down there and built a solid portfolio while she was there, though. She's been back here for a few months now."

Lennox wiped his hands on a napkin.

After a few moments of silence, Preston noticed something in his brother's expression.

"What's up, Ox?"

"What do you mean? Shit's greasy," Lennox said.

"Nah, man. You've got that 'I'm thinking too hard' look and your voice is all pitchy. So, what is it?"

"I'm not overthinking, I'm just..." Lennox looked over and saw the expression on his little brother's face. "Alright, man. I wasn't going to say anything, but... it seems like you might be into her and that's new for me. So, I'm trying to take it all in."

Preston scoffed. "Into her? Bruh, we haven't even spent any real time together."

"That may be true, but I've never heard you go into this much detail about any female—especially one you barely know."

"Well... you know I've dated my share of women who were only interested in what I could do for them. Instead of seeing a young dude who's focused on building his business, they're focused on requesting five-star meals on the first date, expecting me to pull up in a Beamer, and all of that surface shit."

Lennox shook his head. "Yeah, all that nonsense sent me straight into beast mode. Right now, I'm just focused on working hard, traveling, and advancing in my career, not spending time and money on women who won't even last the week."

"Facts. But I'm not quite there yet. I'm still open to finding the right one. Mia's talking about doing something real with her life. She's been hustling to rebuild her business. My long work hours were an issue with other women, but Mia's an entrepreneur, so I don't see her having a problem with it."

Lennox nodded. "That's exactly what you need, bro—someone who gets your mentality, your goals, and what drives you. Someone who respects your grind and what you're trying to build. Hell, you're half Cuban and Black, so you get that hustle gene from both sides."

Preston laughed. "Yeah, no doubt. She reminds me of *mi abuela*—focused, no-nonsense. That's probably why we vibe."

Lennox chuckled. "I ain't half-Latino, but I still know firsthand what that hustle culture's all about."

Preston smiled and dapped him up. "You know it, big bro. Let's get it." There was a brief pause before he spoke again. "Honestly, though, I'm starting to catch feelings for her and shit's a little scary," he admitted. Lennox raised an eyebrow, and Preston continued, "I mean, she's got her own thing going on. She's not like anyone I've been with before. She doesn't need me, and that's a good thing... but it also makes me wonder if I'm enough for her, you know?"

Lennox nodded, leaning back. "I get it, man. Putting yourself out there like that, especially after getting burned in the past, ain't easy. But from everything you're telling me, it sounds like you've found someone worth taking that risk for."

Preston sighed. "Yeah... I keep thinking about mi abuela. She used to tell me that good things don't come easy, but they're always worth it. She never got to see me get my life together, you know? But if she were here, I think she'd tell me to go for it. To stop being scared and start trusting."

Lennox smiled, clapping his brother's shoulder. "Sounds like you already know what you need to do, man. Just take it one step at a time. She's not asking you for anything other than to be yourself."

Preston nodded as his brother's words settled in. "You're right. I just don't want to mess this up. I'm tired of running away from anything real just because it scares me."

"You got this, bro. Trust yourself."

Preston nodded, grateful to have his big brother around for the great advice he always gave.

"So, with all your contacts, you could introduce Mia to new clients," Lennox said.

"You already know. I sent her name out to a few colleagues."

"Hell..." Lennox took a quick swig of water. "I might let her redesign my spot. It could use a feminine touch."

"For what? You know that place stays vacant for most of the year. And when you're in town, you're either camped out at your satellite office or sitting at home playing video games in the dark," Preston chuckled.

"See, that's the last time I go easy on you and let you win. Got you out here with an inflated ego and talking reckless."

Preston laughed. "Man, get outta here with that. But seriously, I appreciate your offer. I'll let her know you're interested and see if she has the capacity to take you on. She's already talking to a few people I've recommended."

"It's no rush, bro. Whenever she gets around to it. I can give you the key if it's after I leave," Lennox said. "I haven't invested much into that place other than a couch, a bed, and a flat-screen. So tell her she can do whatever."

After they left the pizzeria, Lennox ran an errand and Preston headed to the train. On the walk to the train station, he dialed Mia. She picked up on the fourth ring.

"Hello?"

"What's up, Mia? It's Preston."

"Hey, Preston! What's going on?"

"I just grabbed lunch with my brother, Lennox. He's got a one-bedroom apartment over on Rockwell and he's interested in working with you. It's a real bachelor pad, so definitely lower your ex–"

Preston heard a muffled angry voice in the background.

"Tell my man Preston to pay your rent. We're in the middle of a damn meal," a male voice grumbled

"Will you relax? I'm getting off the phone." Mia's tone was sharp.

"Well, hang up, then! This is my time."

"What's wrong with you? You don't tell me what to do."

After a tense pause, Mia took a deep breath. "Preston, I'm sorry. I shouldn't have answered the phone. This isn't a good time. Can I call you back later?"

"No problem. Handle your business," he said, heading down the subway stairs.

Standing on the platform, he replayed what he'd just heard. Just minutes ago, he'd been telling Lennox how different Mia was—how she stood out from every other woman he'd dated. He even saw potential there. He'd barely ever discussed any of the women he'd been interested in with his brother, or anyone else, for that matter.

Now he'd overheard her with some guy, arguing about rent. He sounded super jealous and insecure, so he must have had a reason to be. All of this while he was securing a third client referral for her. He'd even made the full payment for his renovation project to help her out when she'd only asked for a deposit. She'd told him she wasn't seeing anyone, so what were they doing? Was he just another simp she could use to pay her bills?

We can all use extra money around the holidays.

He shook his head as he stepped onto the train. *Man, I can't believe I actually fell for that shit. She had me out here twisted for a minute.* He reached into his pocket and crumpled up her business card which he'd planned to give Lennox. "Well, she doesn't have to worry about me breaking up her little rent hustle. As soon as this contract is wrapped, I'll be out of her hair."

***

Mia stared at the smiling faces of her twin niece and nephew on her phone's home screen in disbelief. Preston had just hung up on her. *What was it with the men in her life lately?*

"Mia!" JoJo growled. "I heard his voice over the phone. You taking calls from dudes while we're together? I guess you no longer need my help. You can just get him to help you out."

She looked up just as JoJo stood and tossed a few folded bills on the table. She hissed, "What the hell? Learn some freakin' manners?"

His eyes narrowed. "What did you say?"

"You heard me. That was a client. Not that I owe you any explanation."

"I'd think you would since this is the second time you're asking me for money. And you're taking calls from a male 'client' during our meal?"

Mia felt heat rising in her chest. "Don't you dare mock me. He was a brand-new client referring another one. You had no right interfering with my conversation. Who the hell are you that I'd feel the need to lie to you?"

He leaned in, lowering his voice. "You're on my time right now."

JoJo's face darkened and Mia was brought right back to the earlier years of their relationship—when he would dangle what he'd done for her, always ready to yank it back if she didn't behave. The memory of all the times she allowed him to make her feel small fueled her fury. She wasn't about to let him think he had any power over her anymore.

"You seem to still have things confused here. I don't belong to you... never have. I don't care what type of help you're offering me." She tapped her temple. "Get that through that thick skull of yours."

He reclaimed his seat, eyes blazing. "Watch that tone."

Mia sat back in her seat and crossed her arms. "Or what? You'll throw another tantrum?"

"Do you need my help or not?"

"Here's one thing you need to know about me, JoJo. I've learned a lot about people like you while I was in Miami. Yes, I'm in a rough spot while trying to get back on my feet right now. Yes, I reached out to you for help out of sheer desperation. But the young girl who allowed you to treat her however you wanted because she relied on you for help is long gone. The gaslighting, threats, and demeaning comments end now. In fact, what am I saying? Screw this."

She tossed her napkin on the table and stood, slipping on her coat before grabbing her purse from the back of her chair.

"Where you think you going?" he hissed through clenched teeth. "We ain't done with this conversation."

"We're not only done with this conversation, we're done co-existing. I can't believe I made the terrible mistake of getting back into this toxic cycle with you. All because I was too stubborn to go to my family for help. I wanted to show them this brand new Mia who was independent, sophisticated, and self-reliant. But I owe myself so much more than lowering myself to accepting this type of treatment from you!"

Mia waited patiently as he sputtered in a pitiful attempt to formulate a response. But he seemed too flabbergasted to gather himself. To think, there was a point when she thought the sun and moon revolved around this man. But her time in Miami taught her the value of hard work and she enjoyed the independence that it introduced into her life. She didn't need another thing from JoJo. She was finally seeing him for the shell of a man he really was. A man who needed to make everyone around him feel small in order to feel good about himself.

She scoffed. "Don't know what to say, huh? Oh, how the mighty have fallen."

Pulling on her hat and gloves, she left the restaurant and stepped out into the crisp air. On the way back to her car, she called Preston back twice, but he didn't answer. Figuring he was tied up with work, she planned to talk to him when she stopped by the office the following week.

When Mia walked the three short blocks from the train stop to A. Gómez Towing several days later, there was a van sitting at the top of the driveway. It didn't have a decal, but she recognized it as a painter's van by the utility shelf and ladder. Once she stepped inside the office, her nose confirmed her suspicion. Plastic tarp covered the floor of the carpeted hallway and painter's tape lined the walls. She didn't see fresh paint or drippings on the tarp, so she followed her nose to the conference room since Trevor wasn't sitting at the front desk. Sticking her head in, she saw the walls were covered in primer. She smiled and said, "Hi, I'm Mia. Are you Oliver?"

A man in navy coveralls was mixing paint in the corner of the room. He looked up and returned her smile. "Yes. Hello, Mia. So nice to meet you in person. Are you looking for Mr. Goméz? They're having a team meeting in the break room since I'll be painting in here."

"Okay, thanks for letting me know." Mia gestured toward

the paint can. "What shade did Mr. Gomez decide to go with?"

"Oh...uh, Morning Sky," he read the label.

"Nice. Well, I'll leave you to it." She headed back down the hall to take a seat in the lobby. She reached into her bag for her pumps and slipped off her walking flats. As soon as she pulled out her phone to check her emails, a melody sounded in her earbuds, signaling an incoming call. She was surprised to see Mr. Hardiman's name on the screen. "Hello?"

"Mia, I'm so glad I caught you. It's not a bad time, is it?"

"Hi, Mr. Hardiman, not at all. How can I help you?"

"Well, I wanted to see if you're still be available for the redesign project of my gallery. I know I initially chose another designer, but he's had a family emergency. Unfortunately, he won't be able to complete the project in the timeframe we originally agreed on."

The memory of being dismissed just because another man seemed more convenient gnawed at Mia as Mr. Hardiman explained. For her, it wasn't just about the money—it was about having a say in her own future, about not letting another man control the opportunities she deserved. She paused, gathering her breath, refusing to let herself be anyone's fallback plan.

Mia frowned. "I'm sorry to hear that. I hope everything's okay."

"Thanks for your concern; he's okay. As I mentioned during our initial meeting, I'm on a pretty tight schedule, and I really need to get started ASAP. Although we didn't get to formally finalize everything, I was very impressed by your portfolio and you came highly recommended."

So now he's impressed and trusts my client's recommendation, she thought. Mia bit her lip, feeling the sting of being his second choice. She had proven her capabilities before, yet Mr. Hardiman didn't even extend her the courtesy of allowing her to reschedule their initial meeting for the next day. Yes, she needed the money, but she wanted to be sure that he was selecting her because of his faith in her ability to do the job.

I'm a lot of things, but someone's substitute ain't one, she thought.

She stood, smoothing her slacks. "I appreciate your call, Mr. Hardiman. I'll need to check my schedule and see what I can move around. How about I call you tomorrow morning?"

"Yes, I completely understand, and I apologize for the short notice. I'm willing to offer you an additional twenty percent over your asking fee, considering the urgency and the inconvenience."

"I appreciate that, Mr. Hardiman. Can you please send over additional details about your desired timeline and your client's art installation in an email?"

"Of course. Just to give you a quick frame of reference, the art installation is for a major client, and we need the gallery ready in just under ten weeks for the unveiling. It's a significant opportunity, and I believe your touch would really enhance the overall experience."

Mia reflected on their initial conversation and quickly did the math in her head. She felt confident that she could pull it off in about nine and a half weeks. Her project management background had taught her to always budget at least three to four weeks of wiggle room in her project schedule. This would be cutting it very close. His original designer had probably given him a leaner schedule and pulled out with a "family emergency" once he realized he couldn't deliver.

"Thanks. I appreciate your call, Mr. Hardiman. I'll give you a call by nine tomorrow."

"Thanks, Mia. Have a good evening."

On shaky legs, Mia reclaimed her seat and released a long breath to calm her nerves. She lowered her shoulders, realizing they'd nearly been touching her ears. Her entire body felt taut and tense. It took her a few moments for her to understand that it wasn't anxiety she felt, but she was livid. She'd allowed two men to make her feel like this in under twenty-four hours with their insensitive demands. Since when did she allow people to walk all over her? She'd studied her ass off and graduated at the top of her class—all while holding down a full-time job and an internship, then picked up and moved to a brand-new city where she didn't know a single soul. So how did she keep finding herself pinned under the thumb of men?

It's because I need this money, she thought. But, all money wasn't good money, especially when her worth was constantly being questioned.

Sniffing, she fished a tissue out of her purse. A few seconds later, she heard a door open down the hall. Preston's was the first voice she heard over the footsteps of a quickly approaching group. She swiped the tissue beneath her nose and took a quick swig from her water bottle before rising to her feet. When he noticed her, his steps faltered, and he stopped mid-sentence.

She locked eyes with him for a moment, expecting a warm welcome, but instead, she was initially met with a cool, distant gaze. Preston's smile was forced and she noticed that his posture was slightly rigid. Mia's heart sank and she fought to conceal her confusion as she turned to flash a smile at Trevor before facing Preston again.

"Preston," she said while trying to inject cheerfulness into her voice to mask her trepidation. "Good afternoon. I hope it's okay that I stopped by for another site visit. I just wanted to ensure that everything's going according to plan. Is this a good time to meet?" She didn't want to mention the reason behind her need to stop by unannounced in front of everyone, which was that he hadn't accepted nor returned her calls.

Preston maintained his forced smile. "Yes, Mia, that works fine. Everyone, this is Mia, our answered prayer. With her guidance and expertise, we'll soon be working in a beautifully renovated office."

The small group smiled and murmured their acknowledgments before dispersing. Mia sensed the discomfort, the underlying tension between her and Preston was apparent. Her heart sank. *What had shifted?* Had he taken her recent calls the wrong way? It seemed like he was pulling away—just when she thought they were getting closer.

But she refused to take another loss today. Straightening her shoulders, she decided to focus on the task at hand. When Preston set off toward his office without another word, she gathered her belongings and followed him.

"Watch your step," he cautioned. "The walls aren't wet, but I don't want your heels to catch in the tarp. It's a total mess, but hopefully, it'll be wrapped up by the end of the day tomorrow."

As Mia passed him to enter his office, she paused to inhale his woodsy cologne. Preston had instinctively extended a protective arm toward her lower back to usher her inside, but she noticed him pull it back just as quickly. Once Preston made it to his desk, she sat across from him. *I guess we're being overly formal now,* she thought, biting her lip.

As they delved into the remaining project details, she cracked a couple of jokes in an attempt to lighten the mood, but Preston's stoic demeanor remained unchanged, leaving the easy camaraderie they once had feeling distant and strained.

Mia requested feedback on the contractors' work and they scheduled a time for her to oversee the furniture and décor installation. Zipping up her attaché case, she said, "We're still on track to wrap this up just under your budget and the proposed timeline looks solid."

"I'm certainly optimistic. Your team has been thorough and professional."

"Thanks for your feedback. It means a lot to me since I'm

pretty much rebuilding my network from scratch at this point."

Preston offered a curt nod, stood, and walked over to his office door with his hands in his pants pockets. Mia nodded in return, but her mind raced, trying to pinpoint what had shifted between them since their evening in the park. She wanted to ask, but bringing up their personal affairs in the office felt inappropriate. Instead, she flashed him one last smile as he thanked her for coming and held the door open.

She stepped out on wobbly legs, fighting the overpowering urge to look back. She thought she'd be able to read him, but she was still no closer to figuring out what had changed.

Now, more than ever, she was determined to prove her capability, not just to Preston but to herself. So, if keeping things strictly professional was the only way forward, she had to accept it. She just hoped she would at least get a strong reference out of it—because clearly, that was all Preston seemed to want now.

Chapter Seven

As soon as the door closed behind her, Preston rushed back to his office before anyone could ask him for anything. He closed the door and immediately began pacing the floor. Mia's impromptu trip to the office had thrown him off. But not nearly as much as those lacy pantyhose, five-inch heels, and royal blue sweater dress that hugged her ample hips.

When those watery brown eyes met his and he noticed those pouty red lips, he had almost lost it. Ignoring her calls had been simple—work had kept him busy with off-site client meetings, job fairs, and renovation updates—but seeing her in person? It messed with his head.

He'd easily worked sixty hours in the last week and the next one promised to be just as active. He'd originally planned to have Trevor reach out to Mia this afternoon regarding his questions. Then she'd shown up looking like a powerhouse. But when he noticed her puffy cheeks, he wanted to walk right over to her, take her in his arms, and threaten bodily harm to whoever had caused her tear tracks. He wanted to assure her that she was safe there with him and had nothing to worry about. But they were no longer in a place where he could say those things to her.

All week long, he questioned whether he'd misread the chemistry between them in the park. He wanted to believe their connection was real. Her body language and pheromones told him that she wanted more than a friendship with him. That kiss had stirred something in him he hadn't felt in years. Mia wasn't just beautiful; she was driven and grounded, the kind of woman who made everyone feel like they had her full attention and no one else in the world mattered. So maybe it had been easy to mistake an innocent connection with a beautiful, smart woman for a spark of irresistible passion.

Then there was the phone call. Hearing that guy in the background telling her to have him pay her rent had pissed him off. He'd been burned before, so he knew what it looked like. And Mia, despite all the charm and chemistry, was starting to look like another potential disappointment. He didn't want to believe it, but he couldn't shake the feeling that she was hiding something from him.

He heard a female voice say, "knock, knock" just before his door opened.

Shelley breezed in, bringing a scent of vanilla and lavender with her. She unbuttoned her pinstripe suit jacket, then took a seat in the plush chair Mia had just vacated, kicking off her heels and crossing her ankles in a single motion. "Hey Prez. Sorry I missed yet another staff meeting. I thought I'd make it back in time."

Preston shook his head at her brazenness and took a seat behind his desk. "Don't worry about that, Shelz. We don't expect our VP of Operations to be here for every meeting. How'd it go with ALG insurance?"

"Very well. I met with the claims department manager and roadside assistance coordinator and they were satisfied with the emergency response procedures, vehicle inspection and regulatory compliance reports you submitted." She sighed and leaned her head against the wall behind her. "This shit's been so exhausting, but we're almost there. Next, we'll all meet to draft a preliminary agreement outlining the terms and conditions of our towing services. Then we'll be ready to start pricing negotiations."

Preston sighed along with her. The regulatory compliance approval process was a huge hurdle that had been weighing on them for weeks. Now that it was behind them, they were almost in the clear. "I'll have Trevor contact Jen to let her know she'll need to attend that meeting," he said, referring to their attorney. "It's not our first rodeo, but it'll be good to have her there during negotiation to spot any red flags and to review the contract."

Shelley nodded, massaging her temples. "Yup, that's what her retainer's for. Do you think we'll be able to handle the capacity of new clients if this goes through? We're already booked solid and hiring new operators left and right."

"*When* this goes through. And yes. Luna and I have been working on expanding the tow operator team. We have a stack of applications from the job fair, so it's just a matter of screening them."

"Well, good luck with that." She began massaging her stockinged feet. "I just peeked into the conference room. That's a really nice color."

"Yeah, it turned out well."

After a few moments, Shelley stood and Preston felt the weight of her piercing stare on the side of his head. "Prez."

"What's up?" he looked up from his laptop screen.

"We were just shooting the shit. Now something suddenly has your undivided attention for the last eight seconds?"

"I was working before you barged up in here."

"Correction: you were pacing like a lunatic up in here."

Preston rolled his eyes. Shelley was just like the little sister

59

he never wanted. "If you must know, I'm updating my calendar for next week, so Trevor has my availability when setting up the meeting with ALG. I suggest you do the same."

"No need," she said, eying her manicure. "My calendar stays ready."

"What day do you think they'll want to meet?"

"The eighteenth is their last day in the office until after the new year. I don't plan to take any time off besides Christmas Eve, Christmas, and New Year's Day."

Preston rolled his eyes. "That's nonsense. We'll be discussing that later, but... cool."

She shrugged. "Why? I don't have any kids or a man and it'll be quiet around here, so I'll actually get some work done."

"Well, hopefully we'll be able to close out the year with a new client on board."

Still staring at the screen, he waited a few minutes for Shelley to leave for her own office, but she stayed put. Reluctantly, he looked up to find her staring at him again.

"Shelz. What's up?"

"Nothing. I just find it weird that you've been raving on and on about how talented this new interior designer is—and I admit, the paint colors are all beautiful and I love the sculptures in the conference and meditation rooms—but now you have nothing to say about her."

"What? I picked out the paint color."

"And she supplied the painter, who's doing a phenomenal job, by the way. I guess I just expected another Mia parade right about now." She did a Miss America wave.

"Yeah, she's good at her job. What more is there to say?"

"Trevor said she was just here and things got pretty awkward."

Preston looked up and scowled. "Yeah? Well, Trevor needs to mind the business that pays him."

Shelley walked over to his office door and closed it.

Leaning against it, she crossed her arms and raised an eyebrow at him. "Really, Gomez? He's not even fifty feet away. Since when do we speak about our employees like that?"

He shrugged and ran a hand over his hair. He knew it was only a matter of time before they had this conversation. But he certainly hadn't expected it to happen less than five minutes after his partner walked into his office.

"What's going on with you? You haven't been yourself for the past few days, plus we've all noticed how you've been working yourself into the ground. You and I vowed to make this a fun workplace for our employees and you've been sucking the life out of this place and making the energy weird around here."

"How would you know? Your ass ain't never here," he snapped.

Shelley's hand flew to her chest in mock offensiveness. "I'm sorry, did you fail to send the memo that closing six-figure deals for us has become a problem?"

Preston fought back a smile.

"Well...? Spit it out. I've known you long enough to realize when something's off with you, so please don't waste time for either of us by continuing with this tough-guy avoidance BS."

Preston started to get defensive but thought better of it. He owed his partner an explanation for his behavior. He sighed, finally closing his laptop. "I don't know, Shelz, it's stupid and complicated."

"Come on now, you know complicated shit's an aphrodisiac for me. Stupidity? More your lane. So go crazy, Gomez."

He stared at his partner for a moment, deciding how much detail to give her. "Things took off pretty quickly with Mia after our first meeting. We grabbed a quick lunch and our evening ended with us kissing in the park."

Although Shelley's eyes reflected her amusement, she didn't say a word.

He continued. "Honestly, I'm feeling her. She's different, Shelz. She's driven, intelligent, and silly. And we've been comfortable around each other from the beginning. It feels like I'm with chillin' with a good friend. Better yet, a fine one."

"Okay, I'm not seeing the problem."

"When I called her the next day, she was out with a guy. Her tone was different, and she rushed me off the phone. Just before we hung up, I heard him tell her, 'have him pay your rent, then.'"

Shelley grimaced. "Oof."

"Right? After we hung up, I started thinking what happened between us wasn't genuine. Like she was just trying to use me to help out with her money issues or–"

Shelley interrupted him with a boisterous laugh.

Preston ran a hand over his face. "Yo, this ain't a joke. I really like her, and it feels like she's keeping something from me."

"Prez, come on. We both know you've been through a lot with women over the years. But it sounds like you're bringing that baggage into your current situation. From what you've been telling me, Mia isn't playing games with you. It seems like she's about her business and she's making moves out here. So, she happened to be with some jealous dude when you called her. How do you know he wasn't another client who just didn't appreciate sharing his time with someone else?"

Preston leaned back in his chair and gazed at the ceiling. "That's not what my gut's telling me."

"Your gut or your fear?" Shelley pushed herself off the door and walked over to his desk. "Look, everyone has stuff going on. Maybe she's not open to sharing all of her messy life details with you just yet. But I suggest talking to her instead of writing her off and jumping to conclusions. Look Prez, I've seen you at your lowest. And I know that you're a good guy who deserves to find happiness. Judging by how she had you strutting around here singing her praises, it seems like Mia's someone you should be trying to get to know better, not pushing away."

He chuckled despite himself. "Strutting around?"

Shelley grinned. "Like a proud little peacock, man. 'Mia said we should do this, Mia recommended that.' Had me wishing this renovation was over before it even started. But seriously, you're overthinking this. We've all got baggage, but don't let yours block your chance at finding something real."

Preston smiled because he knew his friend was happy for him. "It's just hard, Shelz. I've trusted females and I've been burned. It feels like every time I really try to get to know someone, they make me regret it."

Shelley's eyes softened. "Look, if anyone knows how hard this finding love shit is, it's me, Prez. But if she's as different as you say, you need to give her a chance. Talk to her. Get some clarity. Don't push her away because you're scared. If it turns out that she's not into you for the right reasons, fine. But don't sabotage yourself before you even know."

Preston sighed, appreciating Shelley's direct nature for the umpteenth time. It benefited them financially in negotiation meetings, but it also contributed to the trust and love they had for one another. "You always know how to cut through my BS, sis."

Shelley grinned. "Boy, that's just one of many talents. Now, go find Mia. I'll handle the scheduling with ALG."

Shelley was right—he had to stop letting fear cloud his judgment. Whatever was going on between him and Mia, he needed to find out, even if it meant risking disappointment again. He pulled on his pea coat and opened his office door. Just as he was about to leave, Shelley couldn't help herself with one last quip.

"'Using me for my money.' Who the hell do you think you

are, anyway, The Billionaire Bachelor? You dodge your student loan payments one month at a time, just like the rest of us."

Preston held up a middle finger as he left his office. On the way to his car, he pulled up his contacts on his phone, searching for Mia's number. No matter how uncomfortable it might be, he knew there was no turning back. No more guessing, no more overthinking. It was time to get some answers.

Chapter Eight

Mia woke up early and spent the morning cleaning her room and journaling. Whenever she felt anxious, she used journal prompts to clear her mind. Today, she focused on her career, financial concerns, and the sudden shift with Preston. Writing it all out gave her the clarity she needed and she was able to create a new proposal for Mr. Hardiman and prepare for a heart-to-heart with her sister, Arden.

When she knocked on the door and entered her older sister's room, she was greeted by a room full of robust greenery. Each time she visited her sister, Mia felt like she was walking into a jungle. Arden had a money tree, a snake plant, a spider plant, aloe vera, and a bamboo palm all crammed up in her room. She had rescued many of the plants from the neglectful care of their family members. Under the protection of her sister's green thumb, the luscious plants were large, shiny, and thriving.

"Morning. What you up to?" Mia asked, perching on her bed.

Arden's cherry-red lemonade braids fell over her shoulder

as she focused on polishing her toes. Her large, dark eyes took in Mia's outfit from head to toe before returning to the task at hand. "When'd you steal my scarf, thief?"

Mia touched the head wrap decorated with colorful Spanish tiles that pushed her hair back from her face. She'd completely forgotten that she'd snagged it from her sister's room the previous week. "I was just borrowing it for a sec, man. Chill."

Arden shook her head. "If I had a dollar for every time I've heard that one, I wouldn't have to bunk with your broke ass."

"Oop," Mia laughed. "Once a hater, always one."

They sang along with a Becky G. song as Mia leafed through her sister's Free People catalog. After dog-earring a few pages, Mia turned to Arden and whined, "Sisss, I'm having man problems."

Arden rolled her eyes as she cleaned the skin surrounding her toenail with a cotton swab. "What else is newww," she mimicked her.

Mia laughed. "No, really. Remember that guy Preston I was telling you about?"

"Y'all got problems already? Damn, you just met the guy."

"Yes, but I thought it was just a professional relationship. Until we kissed last week, then he started acting all weird and shit." Mia conveniently left out the part about her lunch with JoJo, knowing it would only bring on a hearty lecture from her sister. A woman of few words, Arden was quite verbose when getting Mia told about her screw-ups.

Arden shrugged. "Maybe he wants to keep things professional for now. And that might be for the best, at least until you wrap up his project."

"Yeah, I thought that at first, too. I also thought it may be stress because of a big contract that's on the line for them right now. But he's pulling away completely, and it makes me feel like I did something wrong. Our last meeting was almost a hostile work environment. I couldn't wait to hightail it out of there," Mia said, snagging a chip from her sister's bowl and scooping up salsa. She had it halfway to her mouth before she paused. "You didn't touch these with the same hand you're touching your toes with, right?"

Arden straightened up and deadpanned. "And if I have? That would be my business. These my chips, fool."

Mia crunched on her chip thoughtfully. "So, I should just play it cool until we finish our business together?"

"That's what I would do. Handle your business first. Everything else will sort itself out."

"Sounds like a plan, Stan," she said, standing to leave the room. "You added too many jalapeños to the salsa, by the way." She could barely get her critique out before she was ducking the teddy bear sailing toward her head. Mia ran out of the room and slammed the door behind her just as she heard, "Once again, my salsa, my business, fool!"

Feeling much better after speaking with her sister, Mia did a quick meditation and prayer before picking up the phone. The tone trilled twice before he answered. "Hello."

"Good morning, Mr. Hardiman, it's Mia."

"Hey Mia. Thanks for calling. Once again, I appreciate your willingness to consider taking on my project."

"Of course. So, as promised, I've given the new terms of your project more thought, and while I'm open to helping, there are a few things I'd like to address with you before moving forward. I understand your sense of urgency, but the fact remains that I was your second choice despite my proven track record and references. I know how talented you believed the other gentleman was, but I've seen his online portfolio and he doesn't have nearly as much art industry experience or even close to the total experience I have."

After a brief pause, Mr. Hardiman responded. "I can understand why you feel that way, Mia. But please don't take my previous decision personally. When it came to my choice to book Johnathan, it was nothing more than a right-place, right-time situation. You were both highly qualified, but his supplier and contractor connections here in Brooklyn were just what I needed for my tight deadline. Also, I'd already met with him a week prior to our scheduled meeting. I wanted to get started right away, but my partner insisted that we get a few other quotes first. When you had to reschedule at the last minute, I was still interested in working with you, but time was winding down, so I had to make a tough call."

Mia nodded. "Yes, I understand firsthand how pressing meeting tight deadlines can be. But I need my involvement in your project to be based on the merit of my work, not just because the original designer hit a roadblock."

"Mia, your work speaks for itself. You're a talented visionary and I never doubted your ability to give me exactly what I've envisioned for my space. You have an outstanding portfolio, and I would be honored to work with you on the redesign of my gallery. That is if you'll have me."

Internally, Mia let out a sigh of relief, but she pressed on. The most difficult part of the conversation remained ahead of them. She was determined to reframe the terms of their agreement with confidence and conviction as a professional businesswoman. *You got this,* she thought.

"Thanks for your kind words, Mr. Hardiman. It's good to hear that you value my work, skills, and experience. Additionally, given the depth and complexity of your project, I'll need a revised timeline to juggle my existing commitments while leading your project. Also, considering the last-minute nature of your request, I'll gratefully accept your offer to add another twenty percent over my initial quote. I've outlined how I would approach the expedited timeline in the proposal I sent just before this call."

There was another pregnant pause on his end. Mia willed

herself not to fill the silence as the long, thoughtful seconds slipped by. His hesitation was likely due to her request for more time. It was a big ask—she knew that. But after everything she'd been through recently, she couldn't afford to sacrifice her peace or compromise the integrity of her work. If he couldn't accept her terms, she'd have to walk away.

Her breath caught as Mr. Hardiman finally spoke. "I see. Mia, as I said, I really need your expertise for this. So, I'm willing to do all that I can to meet your terms."

Mia let out a quiet sigh of relief. Arden caught her eye from the hallway, doing a celebratory Milly Rock with champagne in hand. "I knew you'd kill it," she mouthed.

Smiling, Mia turned her back to her sister, vowing to never place another business call on speakerphone while her sister was home. "I really appreciate that, Mr. Hardiman. I want your project to succeed as much as you do, and these adjustments will help me give it my full attention and devotion. I'm happy to finalize the remaining details with you this week so we can get started."

Chapter Nine

Over the next two weeks, Mia transformed Preston's cozy office into a warm, inviting space that felt like a home away from home for employees and a polished, respectable atmosphere for visiting clients. After three long months of struggling, it looked like Mia was finally getting a handle on her finances. Mr. Hardiman eagerly signed a contract and sent a deposit, plus a generous tip. His payment covered two months' rent, leaving Mia with plenty of extra cash for Christmas shopping. Since Preston had also paid her upfront and she'd met several small business owners interested in renovations at a recent networking event, her pipeline looked promising. Mia paid JoJo back with interest—cutting all ties with him for good by sending the money through a certified mail. She'd never been happier to settle a debt.

Mia and Preston had played phone tag for over a week. With demanding work schedules and the holidays approaching fast, they struggled to connect. She spoke to Trevor about the project details and the final walkthrough was scheduled for the first week of the year. She had already shipped Preston a custom gift to show her gratitude, which would arrive just before the end of the year. As such, she was unsure what Preston still needed to speak to her about. As far as she was concerned, there were no loose ends to address.

Nevertheless, Preston had specifically sought her input on furniture that was recently delivered and requested to meet before the walkthrough. The only time she had available was Christmas Eve, and to her surprise, he accepted. After a long day of shopping, Mia changed and headed to A. Gómez Towing.

As she stepped into the office, the transformation still struck her, creating the illusion of added depth in the cozy space. The terracotta walls and modern photography captured the neighborhood's spirit, creating an intimate but professional ambience. Mia kept the soft green in Preston's office and opted for pearlescent cream for Shelley's to capture the natural light to enhance focus and productivity. Fresh poinsettias and strings of soft Christmas lights added a festive feel to the space. Mia smiled, Preston's mom might've had a hand in the holiday decor.

"Hello, Mia."

Preston's voice caught her off guard, pulling her from her thoughts. She turned to find him standing in the hall entryway, dressed in a sleek gray button-down, black slacks, and shiny hard-bottom shoes.

"You look beautiful," he said, stepping toward her with a bouquet of white roses.

Mia smoothed her cream cable-knit sweater dress beneath her red pea coat, trying not to melt under his smoldering gaze.

"Thanks. I'm headed to midnight mass," she said, offering a tight smile as she accepted the flowers. "You look nice too."

She was tempted to close the distance between them, to breathe in his musky cologne, but instead, she kept her composure. "I appreciate these."

Preston's smile softened. "My pleasure. Have you eaten?

My ma made tamales to thank you for your work in the office. She loves how everything turned out."

Mia's stomach growled at the mention of food. "No, I haven't eaten all day. That sounds perfect."

"Come on, follow me."

He led her to the conference room, where the lights were dimmed, and a soft glow from an electric fireplace bathed the room in warmth. A twelve-foot mahogany table with gilded accents stood at the center of the room, surrounded by plush, high-backed leather chairs. The table was covered with a delicate layer of parchment paper, a brass candelabra, a vase of fresh flowers, and an enticing spread of tamales, cilantro rice, and Mexican cornbread.

Mia's mouth watered at the savory answered prayer to her growing hunger pains. She narrowed her eyes at him. "You know you're dirty for this, right? You knew the second you mentioned food, it'd be a wrap for me."

Preston shrugged, a grin tugging at his lips. "No idea what you mean."

"Be sure to thank your mother. She really went all out."

"Will do."

Mia took in the cozy ambiance, thankful she wouldn't have to search for dinner before mass. Preston gestured toward the table. "Please, have a seat."

She glanced around at the decorations and the food laid out before them, the care that had gone into making the evening special. "You know, I've been curious—your company, A. Gómez Towing. The name... what does the A stand for?"

Preston's eyes softened. He took a moment as if gathering his thoughts. "It's for my abuela, Adelina Gómez. She was everything to me growing up. She was just pure love and strength, everything I needed all in one.' He smiled wistfully. "She helped raise me because my ma worked long hours as a corporate attorney. She was a small business owner, so she brought me around her store. She taught me about working hard and never giving up on what I believe in."

Mia smiled. "She sounds amazing. Did she get to see you start this business?"

Preston shook his head, the smile fading slightly. "No... she passed before I got my shit together. I had a rough patch when I was younger—wrong friends and bad decisions. But abuela never gave up on me. When she passed, it was a huge wake-up call. I knew she expected me to do something better with my life. Starting this business was an opportunity to honor everything she valued. This place will always be her legacy."

Mia reached across the table and rested her hand on his. "You're doing an amazing job. I'm sure she'd be so proud of you."

Preston's eyes glistened. "Thanks. Knowing her, she's watching over me to keep me in line. Naming the business after her was my way of making sure her spirit stayed with me every step of the way."

Mia squeezed his hand. "Keep making her proud. Telling from how you are with your team and how you treat people, she's shaped you in innumerable ways."

He looked at her meaningfully, his gaze tender. "Mia, thanks for asking about her. It feels good to share that part of myself."

"Of course," she said. "It was wonderful hearing about Ms. Gómez."

He got up and sat beside her, taking her hands in his. "Look, Mia, I know I've been off lately, and I owe you an apology."

Mia lifted an eyebrow, her silence urging him to continue.

"When I called you the day after our kiss, it sounded like you were with someone... the guy sounded possessive."

"I was out to lunch with my ex, JoJo," Mia explained. "I

borrowed money from him a couple of times. He's not a threat—there's nothing going on between us."

"Well, I can admit... I jumped to conclusions, thinking you were seeing someone else and weren't being honest with me."

Mia shook her head. "Boy, you pole-vaulted clear over common sense."

Preston chuckled softly, lowering his head. "Yeah, I did. I should've talked to you instead of assuming the worst. I've been burned before. Trust doesn't come easy for me, and I let my baggage mess things up between us before we even had a chance."

Mia wanted to be compassionate, but his behavior over the past few weeks hadn't been easy on her. "I understand where you're coming from, Preston. But I've never given you a reason not to trust me. I was hurt that you assumed the worst without bothering to ask me about it."

Preston reached for her hands again and his grip was gentle but firm. "You're absolutely right. I should have given you the benefit of the doubt. I messed up, and all I want is to fix this. Is that what you want?"

Mia studied him for a long moment, weighing his words. He was charismatic, but it was hard to tell if he was being sincere. JoJo, Mr. Hardiman, and now Preston had all been giving her the blues. But something in Preston's eyes, glossy with unshed tears, gave her pause.

He took a deep breath and softened his voice. "I want something different, Mia. I've never seen what a healthy relationship looks like, but I want that with you. The last thing you need is my baggage disrupting your life. I'm finally willing to deal with it so it doesn't become your burden."

Her face softened, but her guard remained intact. She needed to know he was serious about doing the work. "I get that you're asking for grace, but what are you offering me in return?"

Preston's jaw clenched, his eyes never leaving hers. "I'm giving you my word that I'll do better. I'll put in the work because you deserve a much better version of me. I don't want to lose this—whatever it is we have."

Mia held his gaze, her mind racing. She owed him an answer, but the words wouldn't come out.

Chapter Ten

When she looked away, he gently cupped her chin, tilting her face toward him. "Look at me. Please, Mia."

"Preston, you're not the only one who's been through things. I've been hurt by people I trusted too. I just need you to be sure about whether you can trust me."

Preston nodded, his gaze unwavering. "I've never been more confident about anything. I trust you, I adore you, and you've had my utmost respect since day one. I'd be willing to bet everything I have on you being the woman I want to be with."

His eyes held hope and determination, and Mia could see how deeply he meant every word. A tear slipped down her cheek before she could stop it. He reached up and gently swept it away with his thumb. Then he leaned in, pressing a soft kiss to her forehead. "So, is this what you want?"

"Preston, you know it's what I want," she said, her voice breaking.

He shot to his feet, a wide grin spreading across his face as he helped her up from her chair. As soon as she stood, he swept his hand through her hair, cradling the base of her head, and kissed her. It was electrifying; all the pent-up stress and uncertainty from the past few weeks slipped away. She kissed him back hungrily, her fingers gripping the fabric of his shirt as she yanked him closer. She stood on her tiptoes, and his moan vibrated against her mouth as he cupped her behind. After a few intense moments of exploring each other, she pulled away, her breath ragged.

She reached up and swiped her thumb across his swollen lips, wiping away the smear of her red lipstick. "You've got a second chance now," she said, her voice firm but playful. "Don't blow it."

Preston pulled her back in for another quick kiss, this one just as consuming, leaving her breathless. "That's one thing neither of us have to worry about," he murmured against her lips. "I'm going to make you the happiest woman in Brooklyn."

Mia's stomach growled loudly, interrupting the moment. She laughed, pressing her forehead to his. "Well, you can start by feeding me."

He pulled back slightly, looking into her eyes with a serious expression. "I promise, we'll get to the food in a minute. But Mia, listen... I need you to promise me something."

She arched an eyebrow, her smile faltering at his serious expression. "What is it?"

"I want you to be done with asking your ex for money. I don't want you relying on someone like that, especially if he's not treating you right." His eyes held hers, full of concern. "Anything you need—I don't care what it is—you can come to me from now on and I'll help you figure it out. I don't ever want you feeling like you have to go back to that dude for help."

Mia's heart softened at his words, her breath catching. She

could see how genuine he was, how much he wanted to protect her. It wasn't about control for him; he seemed to actually care. "Okay, Preston. I promise. But I need you to know that I won't be asking you for financial help. Figuring things out on my own while rebuilding my business is very important to me. I have an appointment with my bank to apply for a business loan. It's a little scary, but I can't keep plugging all of my personal funds into my business. It's time to bet on myself and let my business stand on its own."

He smiled, his thumb brushing over her cheek. "Mia, I'm so proud of you. I know doing something new like this can be unnerving, but we're in this together now. Just know that you won't be facing anything alone. Not anymore."

She smiled, leaning in to kiss him softly, her heart swelling with gratitude and hope. "I really like the sound of that," she whispered against his lips.

Preston pulled her into a tight embrace, and they stood there for a long moment, holding each other as if sealing their promise.

After a few moments of sweet, slow kisses, Mia said, "Preston?"

"Yeah?" he said, nuzzling his nose into her hair.

"My stomach's touching my back, bruh. I need to eat something before I pass out right here on your newly installed carpet."

"Alright, alright," Preston chuckled, walking her back to the table. He handed her a plate and watched her make a beeline for the tamales. He poured them each a glass of hibiscus tea, and they sat down to eat. They fell into a comfortable silence as they enjoyed the meal. All signs of tension between them had eased into a light and comfortable rhythm.

Once Mia finished eating, Preston asked, "So, did you finish shopping for your niece and nephew?"

She nodded, wiping her mouth. "Yeah, I'm going to walk into their house looking like Señora Claus tomorrow. It felt good to do something nice for them. I've missed so much of their lives while I was away."

"Well, now that you're back, Sofia and Harper can see you anytime they want. Lucky kids."

Mia withered under his warm gaze. Her pulse throbbed in her ears, but she played it cool. Otherwise, this man would have her missing midnight mass doing something that would make Jesus blush. "Thanks... that's sweet."

Preston smiled, reaching for an envelope at the end of the table. "Speaking of gifts..."

Mia shook her head. "Preston, please. You've already fixed my car, patronized my business, given me client referrals, and provided this amazing meal. I can't accept anything else from you."

He shook his head. "Actually, Trevor fixed your car, and ma cooked the meal. And after the small miracle you pulled transforming this place, I couldn't keep you all to myself. Besides, this gift isn't exactly for you. Open it."

Curious, Mia opened the envelope and pulled out a letter. "Harper, thank you for your kind donation to The Children's Heart Foundation. Your donation will support breakthrough congenital heart defect research... "

Mia gasped, her shaky hand flying to her mouth. He'd made a donation of twenty-five hundred dollars in her nephew Harper's name. "Preston, wow..." She stood and threw her arms around him. "Thank you! This means everything to me."

Preston hugged her back. "Turns out this has been a fruitful year for A. Goméz Towing, and Shelley and I couldn't think of a worthier cause to support."

Mia's throat tightened with emotion. "No one's ever done anything like this for me. You've put time into getting to know

79

me, supporting my dreams and my goals. I don't even know what to say."

"Your reaction said it all. And it was my pleasure."

She paused, her eyes glistening as Preston took her hands in his.

"Three weeks ago, when I met with JoJo," she started, her voice trembling. "It was out of desperation. I was facing an eviction, and I was scared. I just wanted to prove I could finally stand on my own two feet, but I realized that my motivation was all wrong. I was moving way too fast and I paid for it. But I'm sorry if I made you feel like what we had wasn't genuine in the process. Because it always has been for me."

Preston squeezed her hands. "I accept your apology, but none of that matters now. We're starting fresh. From now on, it's just us—growing and healing together. Mia, from the moment I met you, I knew you were special. I don't take anything we have for granted. It's me and you from this moment on. Can we agree on that?"

Mia nodded, smiling. "It's a deal."

"Now, I can't promise what the future holds, but I can promise you that I'll never stop trying to get to know you and discovering what makes you happy. And I promise to never let you feel like you're standing alone. Your strength and tenacity are admirable, Mia. I love how fiercely you've fought to stand on your own. But it's okay to let someone stand beside you."

Mia's heart swelled at his words. She'd spent a long time trying to prove something—to her family, to herself—that the idea of someone standing beside her had always seemed like a crutch. But with Preston, it felt different. His words were a gentle embrace, offering a solid promise she could stand on.

Preston reached out, his fingers brushing her cheek as he moved a stray curl from her face. He held her gaze, his voice low and sincere. "You're not just anyone to me, Mia. You're someone who has worked hard, who deserves to be seen, supported, and loved for who you are. I need you to know that you don't have to be alone in this anymore—because I want to be the one standing beside you. And maybe I need that, too. Maybe I need to be the one who's there for you, to share in the good and the bad, to remind us both of what we're capable of when we can rely on someone for unwavering support."

Mia nodded, biting her bottom lip. His words sounded so good. Something deep inside of her was urging her to believe him. To spread her wings, knowing he would be there to cheer her on. It felt foreign, but invigorating.

He stepped to the side and gestured upward, and that's when she saw it—the sparkling mistletoe hanging directly above them. A soft smile spread across his lips. The anticipation of his lips against hers once more was almost overwhelming. Preston leaned in slowly, and she reached for him, pressing her lips to his.

"God Rest Ye Merry Gentlemen" by Andra Day burst through the speakers, jarring them. They pulled apart and Preston broke into a soulful two-step. She laughed, joining him. They moved in sync, spinning and snapping their fingers. As he dipped her, Mia closed her eyes and leaned back. Placing her trust in him was a new feeling. A freeing one.

Right then and there, Mia made the choice to believe in the magic of Christmas again—and most importantly, the choice to believe in herself.

Epilogue

Snowflakes fell gently from the sky as Preston walked up to Mia's apartment with his hands full of grocery bags. He knocked twice, hearing muffled laughter inside. The door swung open, revealing Mia in a bright red apron, her hair tied in messy bun, flour dusting her forehead.

"You made it," she said, stepping aside to let him in. Preston stomped the snow from his boots before walking in. Warm aromas of cinnamon, vanilla, and fresh cookies eagerly greeted him. He set the bags on her kitchen counter, giving Mia a quick kiss on the cheek.

"I brought the extra sprinkles, whipped cream, and vanilla frosting," he said, grinning. "Wouldn't want to disappoint the twins."

Mia smiled. "They're already full of sugar and amped up. Sofia's been asking when you'd get here to help with cookie decorating. She wanted to wait for you."

This would be Preston's second time hanging out with her niece and nephew. They had bonded over candy canes and kettle corn popcorn, so they had already adopted him as their uncle.

Preston smiled. "That's sweet. My little baking buddy."

Just then, Sofia and Harper came running into the kitchen, dressed in matching Christmas PJs. "¡Señor Preston!" the toddlers squealed in unison, wrapping themselves around his legs. Preston laughed, ruffling Harper's hair.

"Hey, Thing One and Thing Two! You guys ready to make the tastiest cookies in all of Brooklyn?"

Sofia nodded vigorously, holding up a cookie cutter shaped like a snowflake. "I make this one for Mommy!"

"Nice choice," Preston said, lifting her up to sit on the counter. "I think she's going to love it."

Harper tugged on Mia's apron. "Tía, red and green sprinkles!"

Mia nodded, her heart swelling at the sight of Preston fitting in so easily with her family. "Great idea, sweetheart."

Once Ari got home, they spent the next hour baking, decorating, and sneaking licks of frosting when they thought Mia wasn't looking. The cozy apartment glowed with Christmas lights and buzzed with the sounds of holiday music, the crackling fireplace, and the children's delighted giggles.

The Christmas tree was tucked away in the corner, out of the way of the energetic twin toddlers. It had been carefully adorned with twinkling lights, and hanging prominently on one of its branches was the elegant ornament Preston had given her, boasting her company's logo. She noticed him staring at it, and she imagined it served as the same reminder she had of how far they had come.

When the cookies were finally ready, they all sat on the living room floor, sipping hot cocoa with mounds of whipped cream, sprinkles, and maraschino cherries. Preston was nestled between Harper and Sofia, tickling them and telling them corny Christmas jokes.

"Señor Preston, you stay at tía's house for New Year's Eve?" Sofia asked with wide, hopeful eyes.

Preston smiled and looked over at Mia, his gaze softening. "If it's okay with your tía."

Mia smiled. "I think that would be perfect."

The children cheered, clapping their sticky hands. Ari helped them wash up and took them into her bedroom to watch a holiday cartoon while Preston and Mia cleaned up the kitchen.

As they washed dishes, Preston leaned over, placing a gentle kiss on Mia's forehead. "Thanks for allowing me to be a part of your new New Year's Eve tradition of making holiday cookies with Harper and Sofia."

"Thanks for spending time with us. Are you ready to meet the rest of the family tomorrow?"

Preston paused, drying his hands on a dish towel before turning to face her. He gave her a soft smile with what seemed to be a mix of excitement and nerves flickering in his eyes. "Ready as I'll ever be. I know they're a bit... particular, and I get it. They're looking out for you, as they should. But I hope they'll see I'm here for the right reasons."

Mia was touched by his sincerity. "They're definitely protective, but once they see how you are with the twins, there's no doubt they'll be Team Preston, just like Ari and Emilia," she said, referring to her sisters.

Preston chuckled. "Well, I've got my charm dialed up to ten just in case."

"Just be yourself, Preston. It's more than enough. My parents can be a little uptight at times, but they can't resist liking someone who makes me happy."

Preston reached for her hand, intertwining their fingers. "And I'm gonna keep doing just that—whatever it takes."

Mia smiled and leaned in, brushing her lips against his, and then whispered, "Then you're already winning."

"Oooh," Sofia and Harper cried, running into the room and covering their eyes.

"Smoochy, smoochy," Harper said, doing a funny dance.

Mia felt her cheeks flush as she cracked up at her niece and nephew.

"Come on, you two. Your mom's walking up now," Arden said, pulling out their coats.

When Emilia—Mia and Ari's sister—arrived to pick up the twins, they hugged Mia and Preston tightly. "Happy New Year, Tia Ari and Mia. Bye, Señor Preston!" they called as they waved goodbye.

Arden retreated to her room with a bowl of popcorn and the apartment fell quiet for the first time in hours. Mia and Preston stood in the living room, the twinkling lights from the Christmas tree casting a warm glow around them. Preston pulled Mia close, wrapping his arms around her waist as they swayed gently to the soft holiday music playing in the background.

"Looks like it's just us." Preston's voice was soft.

Mia smiled, resting her head against his chest. "Yep, just us. I think I like that."

Preston leaned down, his lips brushing against her ear. "This has been one of the best holiday seasons I've had in years."

Mia looked up at him, her eyes glistening. "Same. But it's almost over and we'll be back to the hustle and bustle soon."

"As long as I'm with you, every day is Christmas." He paused as she lifted a brow. After a moment, he said, "You got me watching all these Hallmark Christmas movies. Now I'm talking this corny shit."

With a hand on her chest, Mia asked, "You sure it's my fault? Corniness tends to be an inherited gene, not a learned trait."

He pulled her in for a long kiss. After an hour of being

nestled up on the couch, watching a movie, Mia glanced at the clock.

"It's time," she said.

"Should we grab Ari?" Preston asked, turning on the Times Square countdown.

"Oh no, she's knocked out by eleven every night," Mia said, grabbing the champagne.

As the last minutes of the year slipped away, Preston raised his glass. "Here's to us—to new beginnings, to a new year of happiness, and to every moment we'll share together."

They locked eyes and clinked glasses before enjoying the tingle of the chilled champagne.

"So, Mr. Goméz, do you have a resolution?" Mia asked.

Preston looked down at her, a smile tugging at his lips. "To keep my promise of making you the happiest woman in Brooklyn."

Mia's eyes glistened as she looked up at him. "Oh yeah? Well, my resolution is to let you."

The countdown began, and as the crowd chanted, Preston pulled Mia even closer on the couch.

"Three... two... one..."

Preston leaned down, pressing his lips to hers.

In that kiss was everything they'd promised, everything they'd worked for. There was vulnerability, hope, and summoning the courage to trust again.

Preston pulled away slightly, resting his forehead against her, their breath mingling in the shared space between them. His thumb brushed along her cheek as if memorizing the curve of her face, his eyes searching hers.

"Happy New Year, Mia," he whispered, his voice laced with warmth.

Mia smiled, gently cupping the back of his neck. "Happy New Year, Preston."

They snuggled up and he reached for the remote. When

his phone pinged, he looked down at the screen and tapped on it. Grinning, he looked at her. "Well, well. If it isn't a five-star review of A. Goméz Towing from Mia Reyes."

Returning his smile she said, "I scheduled it to be the first one of the new year."

"Well, thanks. I'm sure this will be a year full of firsts for us," he said, pulling her in for a hug. "I can't wait to experience them with you."

As they pulled away, Mia's eyes shone with hope. "No more walls," she whispered, her throat tight with emotion.

Preston nodded, his voice steady. "No more walls. Just us."

They held each other close, knowing that whatever came next, they had each other's backs—all while trusting, hopeful, and ready for wherever their newly joint path would lead them.

Author's Note

Mia and Preston's story began in my debut novel, *Beauty Beheld*. They quickly became fan favorites, and my readers insisted they get their own story—leading to the creation of *Mistletowed*. Since the *Beauty Is Her Name* series centers around Patience and Lennox, I decided to tell Mia and Preston's origin story in a holiday novella.

I love writing stories about Black love, and that includes celebrating the full spectrum of the Black diaspora. Whether it's Black and Latino, Black and white, or other multicultural pairings, these love stories are all part of the bigger picture of our experience.

In *Beauty Betrothed*, the sequel to *Beauty Beheld*, you'll get a much closer look at each of these couples, and I can't wait for you to see what's next for them.

Follow me on social media @AuthorZariahLBanks to stay updated on the next installment in the *Beauty Is Her Name* series.

Zariah L. Banks

Acknowledgments

Thanks to my hubbae, Doug, for always protecting my writing time while we're raising these bambinos.

Thanks to Michael C. Payne (Mike), for always being my trusty beta reader, developmental editor, typesetter–whatever I need, you got me. I'm grateful for my beta reader team: Maria, Cheryl, and Natassha. Your feedback and input were invaluable in the final hour, as I was far too close to this story to catch everything. As my tribe, you are unmatched and I love you all.

Special shout-outs to The Book Club and The Bookish Brunch Club for being early readers of Mistletowed. Your feedback and support mean everything.

To anyone who's found inspiration to heal emotional wounds, self-advocate, and renew their pursuit of love because of these pages, I thank you for spending time with this book. I also thank you in advance for sharing it with others.

Hugs,

ZLB

About the Author

Multi-award-winning emotional intimacy novelist Zariah L. Banks tells stories about beautifully flawed people who are often victims of unrequited love. She is best known for *Beauty Beheld*, the first title in the *Beauty is Her Name* series, and the Amazon bestselling holiday short, *Mistletowed*. Beauty Beheld was a featured title in the Indie Author Project Select collection, a collection of the best indie books in the Indie Author Project program on Biblioboard.

Zariah loves book clubs! As an avid book club member for most of her adult life, she would love a personal invite to attend yours. For a free Book Club Discussion Guide complete with an appetizer menu and relationship Q & A's, or to request an in-person or virtual author appearance for your book club discussion of *Beauty Beheld or Mistletowed*, please fill out a book club request form at ZariahLBanks.com/book-clubbae

For more tips on establishing self-love and emotional intimacy, and finding the love of a lifetime, visit her blog at www.ZariahLBanks.com/main-blog and follow her on social media at @authorzariahlbanks on Instagram & TikTok and ZariahLBanks_ on X

Made in the USA
Columbia, SC
20 November 2024